NEVER

TELL

(A May Moore Suspense Thriller —Book Two)

BLAKE PIERCE

Blake Pierce

Blake Pierce is the USA Today bestselling author of the RILEY PAGE mystery series, which includes seventeen books. Blake Pierce is also the author of the MACKENZIE WHITE mystery series, comprising fourteen books; of the AVERY BLACK mystery series, comprising six books; of the KERI LOCKE mystery series, comprising five books; of the MAKING OF RILEY PAIGE mystery series, comprising six books; of the KATE WISE mystery series, comprising seven books; of the CHLOE FINE psychological suspense mystery, comprising six books; of the JESSE HUNT psychological suspense thriller series, comprising twenty four books; of the AU PAIR psychological suspense thriller series, comprising three books; of the ZOE PRIME mystery series, comprising six books; of the ADELE SHARP mystery series, comprising fifteen books, of the EUROPEAN VOYAGE cozy mystery series, comprising four books; of the new LAURA FROST FBI suspense thriller, comprising nine books (and counting); of the new ELLA DARK FBI suspense thriller, comprising eleven books (and counting); of the A YEAR IN EUROPE cozy mystery series, comprising nine books, of the AVA GOLD mystery series, comprising six books (and counting); of the RACHEL GIFT mystery series, comprising six books (and counting); of the VALERIE LAW mystery series, comprising three books (and counting); of the PAIGE KING mystery series, comprising six books (and counting); and of the MAY MOORE suspense thriller series, comprising three books (and counting).

An avid reader and lifelong fan of the mystery and thriller genres, Blake loves to hear from you, so please feel free to visit www.blakepierceauthor.com to learn more and stay in touch.

BOOKS BY BLAKE PIERCE

MAY MOORE SUSPENSE THRILLER
NEVER RUN (Book #1)
NEVER TELL (Book #2)
NEVER LIVE (Book #3)

PAIGE KING MYSTERY SERIES
THE GIRL HE PINED (Book #1)
THE GIRL HE CHOSE (Book #2)
THE GIRL HE TOOK (Book #3)
THE GIRL HE WISHED (Book #4)
THE GIRL HE CROWNED (Book #5)
THE GIRL HE WATCHED (Book #6)

VALERIE LAW MYSTERY SERIES
NO MERCY (Book #1)
NO PITY (Book #2)
NO FEAR (Book #3

RACHEL GIFT MYSTERY SERIES
HER LAST WISH (Book #1)
HER LAST CHANCE (Book #2)
HER LAST HOPE (Book #3)
HER LAST FEAR (Book #4)
HER LAST CHOICE (Book #5)
HER LAST BREATH (Book #6)

AVA GOLD MYSTERY SERIES
CITY OF PREY (Book #1)
CITY OF FEAR (Book #2)
CITY OF BONES (Book #3)
CITY OF GHOSTS (Book #4)
CITY OF DEATH (Book #5)
CITY OF VICE (Book #6)

A YEAR IN EUROPE

A MURDER IN PARIS (Book #1)
DEATH IN FLORENCE (Book #2)
VENGEANCE IN VIENNA (Book #3)
A FATALITY IN SPAIN (Book #4)

ELLA DARK FBI SUSPENSE THRILLER
GIRL, ALONE (Book #1)
GIRL, TAKEN (Book #2)
GIRL, HUNTED (Book #3)
GIRL, SILENCED (Book #4)
GIRL, VANISHED (Book 5)
GIRL ERASED (Book #6)
GIRL, FORSAKEN (Book #7)
GIRL, TRAPPED (Book #8)
GIRL, EXPENDABLE (Book #9)
GIRL, ESCAPED (Book #10)
GIRL, HIS (Book #11)

LAURA FROST FBI SUSPENSE THRILLER
ALREADY GONE (Book #1)
ALREADY SEEN (Book #2)
ALREADY TRAPPED (Book #3)
ALREADY MISSING (Book #4)
ALREADY DEAD (Book #5)
ALREADY TAKEN (Book #6)
ALREADY CHOSEN (Book #7)
ALREADY LOST (Book #8)
ALREADY HIS (Book #9)

EUROPEAN VOYAGE COZY MYSTERY SERIES
MURDER (AND BAKLAVA) (Book #1)
DEATH (AND APPLE STRUDEL) (Book #2)
CRIME (AND LAGER) (Book #3)
MISFORTUNE (AND GOUDA) (Book #4)
CALAMITY (AND A DANISH) (Book #5)
MAYHEM (AND HERRING) (Book #6)

ADELE SHARP MYSTERY SERIES
LEFT TO DIE (Book #1)
LEFT TO RUN (Book #2)

LEFT TO HIDE (Book #3)
LEFT TO KILL (Book #4)
LEFT TO MURDER (Book #5)
LEFT TO ENVY (Book #6)
LEFT TO LAPSE (Book #7)
LEFT TO VANISH (Book #8)
LEFT TO HUNT (Book #9)
LEFT TO FEAR (Book #10)
LEFT TO PREY (Book #11)
LEFT TO LURE (Book #12)
LEFT TO CRAVE (Book #13)
LEFT TO LOATHE (Book #14)
LEFT TO HARM (Book #15)

THE AU PAIR SERIES
ALMOST GONE (Book#1)
ALMOST LOST (Book #2)
ALMOST DEAD (Book #3)

ZOE PRIME MYSTERY SERIES
FACE OF DEATH (Book#1)
FACE OF MURDER (Book #2)
FACE OF FEAR (Book #3)
FACE OF MADNESS (Book #4)
FACE OF FURY (Book #5)
FACE OF DARKNESS (Book #6)

A JESSIE HUNT PSYCHOLOGICAL SUSPENSE SERIES
THE PERFECT WIFE (Book #1)
THE PERFECT BLOCK (Book #2)
THE PERFECT HOUSE (Book #3)
THE PERFECT SMILE (Book #4)
THE PERFECT LIE (Book #5)
THE PERFECT LOOK (Book #6)
THE PERFECT AFFAIR (Book #7)
THE PERFECT ALIBI (Book #8)
THE PERFECT NEIGHBOR (Book #9)
THE PERFECT DISGUISE (Book #10)
THE PERFECT SECRET (Book #11)
THE PERFECT FAÇADE (Book #12)

THE PERFECT IMPRESSION (Book #13)
THE PERFECT DECEIT (Book #14)
THE PERFECT MISTRESS (Book #15)
THE PERFECT IMAGE (Book #16)
THE PERFECT VEIL (Book #17)
THE PERFECT INDISCRETION (Book #18)
THE PERFECT RUMOR (Book #19)
THE PERFECT COUPLE (Book #20)
THE PERFECT MURDER (Book #21)
THE PERFECT HUSBAND (Book #22)
THE PERFECT SCANDAL (Book #23)
THE PERFECT MASK (Book #24)

CHLOE FINE PSYCHOLOGICAL SUSPENSE SERIES
NEXT DOOR (Book #1)
A NEIGHBOR'S LIE (Book #2)
CUL DE SAC (Book #3)
SILENT NEIGHBOR (Book #4)
HOMECOMING (Book #5)
TINTED WINDOWS (Book #6)

KATE WISE MYSTERY SERIES
IF SHE KNEW (Book #1)
IF SHE SAW (Book #2)
IF SHE RAN (Book #3)
IF SHE HID (Book #4)
IF SHE FLED (Book #5)
IF SHE FEARED (Book #6)
IF SHE HEARD (Book #7)

THE MAKING OF RILEY PAIGE SERIES
WATCHING (Book #1)
WAITING (Book #2)
LURING (Book #3)
TAKING (Book #4)
STALKING (Book #5)
KILLING (Book #6)

RILEY PAIGE MYSTERY SERIES

ONCE GONE (Book #1)
ONCE TAKEN (Book #2)
ONCE CRAVED (Book #3)
ONCE LURED (Book #4)
ONCE HUNTED (Book #5)
ONCE PINED (Book #6)
ONCE FORSAKEN (Book #7)
ONCE COLD (Book #8)
ONCE STALKED (Book #9)
ONCE LOST (Book #10)
ONCE BURIED (Book #11)
ONCE BOUND (Book #12)
ONCE TRAPPED (Book #13)
ONCE DORMANT (Book #14)
ONCE SHUNNED (Book #15)
ONCE MISSED (Book #16)
ONCE CHOSEN (Book #17)

MACKENZIE WHITE MYSTERY SERIES
BEFORE HE KILLS (Book #1)
BEFORE HE SEES (Book #2)
BEFORE HE COVETS (Book #3)
BEFORE HE TAKES (Book #4)
BEFORE HE NEEDS (Book #5)
BEFORE HE FEELS (Book #6)
BEFORE HE SINS (Book #7)
BEFORE HE HUNTS (Book #8)
BEFORE HE PREYS (Book #9)
BEFORE HE LONGS (Book #10)
BEFORE HE LAPSES (Book #11)
BEFORE HE ENVIES (Book #12)
BEFORE HE STALKS (Book #13)
BEFORE HE HARMS (Book #14)

AVERY BLACK MYSTERY SERIES
CAUSE TO KILL (Book #1)
CAUSE TO RUN (Book #2)
CAUSE TO HIDE (Book #3)
CAUSE TO FEAR (Book #4)
CAUSE TO SAVE (Book #5)

CAUSE TO DREAD (Book #6)

KERI LOCKE MYSTERY SERIES
A TRACE OF DEATH (Book #1)
A TRACE OF MURDER (Book #2)
A TRACE OF VICE (Book #3)
A TRACE OF CRIME (Book #4)
A TRACE OF HOPE (Book #5)

PROLOGUE

Danny Charter stood by the shores of Eagle Lake, Minnesota, staring out in a calculating way across the waters. It was a beautiful early summer evening, just starting to get dark, but his mind was not on the aesthetic details of this serene view.

Instead, his brain was busy with the ways to get maximum value from the build of the hotel's new wing, in this attractive setting, while also capitalizing on the surroundings.

He paced the shore, ideas for the build flooding his mind.

Proximity to the lake would be first prize, but of course one had to take flood lines into account. It became expensive to raise the foundations. And while he personally thought it was okay to encroach on wetlands, there were always those residents and environmental groups who'd start shrieking and screaming, and not all officials would overlook it. Bribery was part of the package but one didn't want to overspend in that direction.

The locals in Tamarack County mostly hated progress. A backward lot, they complained about everything, from ruining the environment to breaking the zoning laws. They complained about the traffic and the increase in rates and taxes that progress would bring, and the noise.

He was likely to spend more time fending off their ridiculous objections than he was planning the actual build.

He rubbed his chin thoughtfully—then a cracking noise from behind made him jump.

He glanced around, looking dubiously at the thick, dark woodlands.

He'd heard this area of the shore, being more isolated, could be dangerous in terms of wildlife. Coyotes, even bears.

Danny shivered at the thought of being attacked by a rabid coyote. That kind of thing was rife out here in the countryside.

All he needed was to be attacked by a bear, while out of range of the safety and comfort of his BMW, parked at the end of the blacktopped part of the road. Not wanting to get it dirty, he'd walked the rest of the way.

Now, he was starting to realize how far from his car he was. Suddenly, this area felt a lot more threatening. It was strange how the entire atmosphere changed as night fell, he thought uneasily. What had been scenic and rural swiftly became dark and unfriendly.

And he really wanted to know what that noise was. It was a rustling, but it was louder than he thought it should be for a small animal.

He swallowed, his throat dry.

His hand dropped to his belt, to feel the reassuring shape of the pepper spray. If any wildlife attacked him, they'd soon regret it, he told himself.

From somewhere, he remembered that if a bear was approaching you should shout. Show aggression. Intimidate it.

Danny liked that line of thinking; it fit with his ethos.

"Scoot, bear!" he yelled. Whatever wildlife was lurking around needed chasing off. "Hiya! Get going!"

It was a little hard to keep his voice booming when he felt this unsure, but he did his level best.

There was a pause, then another crashing sound.

He felt relieved. His shout had clearly scared the wildlife away. He rubbed his hands together, triumphant. Nothing to worry about.

He turned around, using the proposed lobby as his starting point, and trod out the distance.

Precise measurements would be done in the next few days. He just wanted it clear in his own mind where the building would start and end, and if it would fit within the terrain.

A noise came behind him again, and wrapped in his own thoughts, counting the numbers, he was too slow to react.

It hadn't been the bear noise this time. It was more like footsteps, running fast behind him.

And then, just as his mind was starting to realize this might be very wrong, he felt something bludgeon him over the head.

Danny staggered, stars exploding in his vision, dropping to his knees. He felt dizzy. Something, someone, had attacked him from behind.

He struggled to rise, but it was impossible.

He was moving.

Dimly he realized he was being dragged down the grassy bank where he'd so recently decided the flood line could safely be ignored.

Bump, bump, bump.

The world grayed out, but Danny was aware of cold water surrounding him. And strong hands, holding him down.

He opened his mouth to scream, but the hands were too strong, the pressure on his head too intense. The water covered him, cold and dark.

He struggled as the hands pressed down and the water rushed into his lungs. But he was no match for his attacker's strength, and he needed air.

Gasping in a breath, he felt a choking surge of cold water rush down his throat.

Danny felt dimly aware of the fact that he had been a fool. He should never have come here, alone, at night. If only he'd done his pacing earlier, in the daylight.

The dark waters closed over his head, and the last thing Danny saw was the gleam of moonlight on the water, reflecting back his startled face as he sank into its depths.

CHAPTER ONE

Deputy Sheriff May Moore stood in the evidence room. It was a narrow, long room located at the back of the Fairshore police department's main building.

It was well secured, with thick walls and no windows. There was a ventilation grille high in the wall, and ceiling lights. In winter it was a freezing place, but in summer it was pleasantly cool.

It was eight a.m. on an early summer morning now, and May felt the chill as she carried an item inside, to add it to one of the current cases. Now that she'd been promoted to deputy, organizing and maintaining this evidence room was one of her new tasks.

The walls were lined with shelves, on which the evidence from the cases was neatly stored in date order.

Pushing a strand of sandy blond hair back from her face, she leaned down, placing the item, in its plastic evidence bag, on the correct shelf.

Here, in this room, decades of items from past crimes were stored, waiting to be brought out and used as evidence against the criminals. Mostly, in this quiet town, on the shores of Eagle Lake in Tamarack County, Minnesota, these crimes were not serious. This one was from a burglary. The burglar had dropped a Kleenex from his jacket pocket as he'd stuffed valuables into them. Even used Kleenexes could provide vital forensic evidence. This one had just come back from analysis and would now be stored here.

Sometimes, May thought she could feel the weight of the past crimes in the room. There was history here. Unsolved crimes. Cold cases that filled her with concern when she thought about the criminals still at large.

And all the way at the end of the room was the box containing the evidence from her sister's disappearance.

Holding her breath, May paced down the well-swept floor to the far end of the evidence room. As she walked, she could see the boxes looked older, smelled mustier.

Her heart pounded hard as she reached the box where the meager evidence from her sister's disappearance ten years ago was stored away.

At the age of eighteen, Lauren had gone missing after storming out of the house, following a fight with nineteen-year-old May. That fight always made May feel desperately guilty. If they hadn't fought, would her sister be here today?

She'd gone down to the lake. Witnesses had seen her walking that trail.

And May knew that a bloody scrap of fabric,, one that matched up with the top she'd been wearing, had been found snagged on a shrub near the pier.

Her body had never been found.

Since then, they had been two sisters, not three. May, and her older sister, Kerry. Kerry had always been the golden child, the most successful, the highest achiever, doted on by her parents. Today, she was an FBI agent with a brilliant career, embodying her parents' dreams. May had always lived in her shadow.

She often wondered if the dynamic would have been different if Lauren had still been alive.

If only she knew what had happened, what had played out on that terrible day. There might be other things in the box. What if there were? May had never seen the contents. Sheriff Jack, her boss, had not been in charge back then. There had been an older sheriff heading up this precinct, who'd retired two years after Lauren had vanished.

There it was. May stood, facing the box that contained all traces of her sister's investigation, breathing in its musty smell, wondering what else was in it.

Just a couple of weeks ago, Sheriff Jack had given her permission to look at Lauren's case. May felt desperate to know if there was any detail that had been overlooked. Perhaps some crucial piece of evidence had been missed, and now that she was county deputy, she might have the reach and the responsibility to be able to take it further.

But to May's consternation, opening a case was not a quick process. Wheels had to be put in motion. Records and paperwork had to be requested from the archives, which were not stored on site, but in the main police department in Misty Hills. Nothing could be done until the correct permissions had been granted and all the information had been collated.

It was all frustratingly slow, and meanwhile this box stood literally within arm's reach of her.

May reached out her arm and touched it, running her fingers over the cardboard, seeing the faint traces of dust.

She knew if she opened the box, she would be putting herself in the heart of the past. She traced the outline of the lid where it had been taped shut.

It seemed to beckon to her.

What was inside? She didn't even know. Could there be a clue in here that could change everything?

She didn't know, but she suspected the contents of the box would be a stark reminder of the reality of her sister's disappearance. She was sure painful memories would surge.

And yet she couldn't open it. Not until the paperwork had been scanned and sent over, and until Sheriff Jack had the official confirmation that this case was active again.

How she wished she could grab the box out of this room, take it home, and peek inside. Nobody would know or care if she did. The only person going into this room at the moment was her.

For a moment, the voice of temptation was loud and persuasive.

If there was anything vital to be found that could help her find out more about what had befallen her sister, it might be in here. Perhaps there would even be evidence that a cold-blooded killer was still out there somewhere. The contents of this box might lead her to the heart of it.

For a moment, May actually slipped her hands around the box and lifted it, feeling its weight. It wasn't a heavy box. It was average size, only about eighteen square inches. Just a moment or two alone in this room, and she could take the tape off and see—actually see—what was inside.

May sighed.

She couldn't do it. She didn't have it in her to misuse her position in that way. No matter how much she longed to glimpse what was inside, she knew she couldn't. She was not that person. In fact, she needed to get out of this room before she was tempted to do something she'd regret for the rest of her life.

She had a busy day, and she told herself firmly that there was no point moping around the evidence room, mooning over boxes that she was not allowed to open.

She had to focus on her job, and not pilfer evidence boxes for selfish reasons, looking for the tiniest ray of hope, or at least closure, on the terrible event that had defined her life since then.

May sighed. Sometimes, being a law enforcement officer was harder than it seemed, but she'd determinedly done her best ever since joining, and she was going to do her best now.

As she stood there, still strangely conflicted, she reminded herself of the oath she'd taken when she'd first joined the police.

"I will protect and serve with every breath in my body."

And so she would.

She was May Moore, Deputy Sheriff of Tamarack County. Even if the evidence room held secrets that could break her.

Putting the box carefully back on the shelf, she turned away.

As she left the room, locking the door behind her, she heard Sheriff Jack call her name loudly. May jumped, feeling guilty even though she'd done no more than hold that old box for a few moments. Had Jack seen? Did he know?

"Yes, Sheriff?" she asked quickly, as she hurried back into their shared office.

But he wasn't sitting at his desk. The gray-haired, pleasant-faced sheriff was standing at the door, and his next words brought clarity—as well as a speeding up of her heart.

"May, we need to head down to Eagle Lake urgently. A body's just been found there."

CHAPTER TWO

May grabbed her purse from her desk and raced out of the office, hot on Jack's heels. A body at the lake?

The memory of her recent case flashed into her mind. A serial killer had captured young women, holding them locked away before killing them and dumping them in the lake.

May had solved that case, which had been brutal and terrifying. Now, the news of another body made her blood chill.

Perhaps it was a drowning, an accident, death by misadventure. Sad though that would be, at least it would mean that someone hadn't taken someone else's life.

Such things rarely happened in this quiet town, but as May knew all too well, evil could lurk anywhere.

She could see from the grim set of Sheriff Jack's mouth that he felt the same as he climbed into his cruiser. May jumped in the passenger side and they sped away. The early morning traffic, such as it was, had already dissipated and May knew they wouldn't need to turn on the siren for this short drive.

"Do they know what happened? Are the circumstances suspicious?" May asked.

"The coroner is on site now. It's not in Fairshore itself. This is a couple of miles away. I believe it's not far from the site of that new hotel."

"Oh, the Lakeside Heights?" May frowned. Anything to do with Lakeside Heights was going to be bad news, she just knew it.

The hotel had recently been built, despite numerous objections, on the road between Fairshore and the neighboring town to the east, Chestnut Hill.

"Yes, that one." Jack's tone told her he felt the same.

Construction of the hotel had wrapped up a few months ago, and May had been inundated with complaints during the process. It seemed that one or other of the surrounding police had been called out there on a daily basis.

If it wasn't violation of the stipulated building times, it was noise issues, trucks using roads that weren't up to their weight limit, building rubble being illegally dumped, or accidents on the road that the builders had failed to report.

On the first night of the opening party, which had been a few weeks ago, May had been called there twice. Once, it was because of a fight in the parking lot, and once because of a drunk and disorderly person.

She had wondered if there would be any more of these incidents in the future.

And now, apparently, there was a dead body near this site.

Could it be related to the construction? To the huge amount of fuss that had been made during it? May knew tempers had flared, and locals had been seriously angry about this new development.

She felt a tingling of fear as she saw the lake come into view. It was scenic, a massive expanse of calm water, fringed by wood and grassland. Beautiful though it was, May didn't like it at all. The memories of Lauren's disappearance were too intense. She never went near the lake unless she had to.

There was the hotel, its bulk cutting into the skyline ahead of them. And there, beyond it, May saw the flashing blue and red lights that signaled where emergency services were stopped. It was near the old pier, which was a quirky wooden structure full of character that had been in the area for decades and was a well-loved landmark. Of course, she understood the hotel planned to demolish it during the second phase of their build.

She climbed out of the car and hurried over. A scuba diver was surfacing from beneath the lake's blue, lapping surface. He waded to shore.

"I can't see anything else down there. No other bodies, and no other items or possessions," he said.

That voice was familiar, May thought in surprise.

Wading further out of the lake, the tall, lean diver made his way over to them and May saw that it was none other than Deputy Owen Lovell, her investigation partner.

"Owen!" she exclaimed. "You're a diver?"

"Yes," he admitted, with a sheepish grin, shaking water out of his short, dark hair. "I did a course in my teens and I've kept up to date ever since."

"I had no idea!" she said.

Thirty-year-old Owen had joined the police two years ago, quitting the accounting firm he'd worked for to pursue a career that made more of a difference. A year ago he'd transferred to May's precinct and been assigned as her partner.

She'd been surprised a few times in the past year by his talents in unexpected directions. This was definitely one of them.

"The victim was stuck under the jetty. I think a current lodged him there. He was fully clothed, wearing a business suit, and had his shoes on." Owen sounded serious.

"Who saw him?" May asked.

"A fisherman and his son who arrived in the early morning. They noticed something that looked suspicious in the water and called the police immediately. They then went back home. The father didn't want his son to wait around if it was a body."

May exchanged a glance with Jack. Who was this fully dressed, mysteriously drowned man?

They paced over to the knot of people surrounding the recovered body.

Immediately, May recognized the pathologist Andy Baker. He was examining the body.

He stood up and turned to them, and she could already see on his face that this was not going to be a routine drowning. If the victim being fully clothed hadn't clued her, Andy's expression did.

"I'm afraid we might have foul play here," he said. "I'm not sure as yet, but we must be prepared for the possibility."

May's heart sped up.

First things first, she told herself.

"Do we have an ID on the victim?" she asked.

"Yes, we do," Andy said. "He's Danny Charter. The hotel's architect. He had ID on his person, in his wallet. And his vehicle is parked near the road."

May glanced around.

Sure enough, a large, black BMW was parked nearby, the paintwork still covered in dew.

"If he's been in the water overnight, it ties in with residents' reports that this car was here last night," Jack said.

May was trying to piece together what could have happened.

"What's the cause of death?" she asked, needing to finalize the most important piece of this puzzle.

"He has a head injury. He was struck, or fell, causing a deep injury to the back of his head. From there, he drowned. I can't see any other injuries, though. He doesn't seem to have any defensive wounds," Andy explained.

"Could he have fallen off the pier?" Jack asked. "The victim could have hit his head on an object, or a rock in the water, before he drowned."

May thought that was a good theory. She wasn't sure what he could have hit his head on, though. That was the problem. There was nothing obvious in sight.

"It's unlikely, but it is possible," Andy agreed. "Cause of death was drowning, but the head injury could have been the cause of that."

May stepped forward to take a look at the dead body, steadying herself inwardly before she stared down. She didn't have a lot of experience with murder. Taking a look at a corpse was always a shocking sight.

The victim looked to be in his thirties, with short brown hair. He was dressed in what she thought was a designer suit, with a black shirt and smart black shoes, one of which was placed by the body. She guessed Owen had dived for it. His face was sheet white, his eyes open.

What was it? Murder or misadventure?

Staring at the body, May wished she knew for sure.

Had someone deliberately murdered the architect of a hotel that was already the center of controversy and contention? This would be potentially disastrous. The scenic towns surrounding Eagle Lake were only just beginning to recover from the recent serial killer case that had ripped through the communities. Now, another person had been killed?

With her mind reeling in disbelief, May knew this incident would end up reflecting badly on the town's policing. If this was not solved immediately, people were going to be looking for a scapegoat, for someone to blame as panic surged. As the recently promoted county deputy, she would have to shoulder the criticism and provide the answers.

"We need to get photos of the body, the scene, and the surroundings," May said to Jack, as the police photographer got out of his car and hurried down to the scene.

And then her eyes narrowed as she saw something strange. Something that didn't look right.

"What's that?" she asked, pointing down to the dead man's throat.

11

CHAPTER THREE

"What are you looking at?" Andy Baker asked May. She pointed more closely.

"It looks as if there's something stuck in his mouth. Right at the back of his throat. You can actually see the bulge in his windpipe. I was wondering, could he have choked, somehow?"

"You're right," Andy said. "There is something there."

May stepped back to let him examine it more closely. The wind from the lake tugged at her hair. It was cool and fresh. It smelled of pine and clean air. Again she thought how strange and wrong it was that this man was lying here, after having drowned in these pristine waters.

A few locals were already standing and watching, keeping well back from the crime scene tape. May saw a couple of dog walkers, a jogger who was doing stretches against a wooden bench while staring down at the lake, and also a couple of uniformed staff who looked to have walked over from the hotel's premises.

Andy crouched down by the body and gently opened the victim's lips wider.

He moved the body's head to one side. Then he drew a sharp breath as he saw what was stuck in the dead man's mouth.

"It's a piece of paper," he said, sounding intrigued.

May squatted next to him, peering closer.

Andy took out a pair of tweezers and gently teased the paper out of the dead man's mouth. He opened it with his gloved hands.

"It's a five-dollar bill," he said in even more incredulous tones.

"Crumpled up in his throat?" May asked. This was totally confusing and not what she'd expected at all.

"Yes." Andy's voice was hard. "I'm sorry to say but this adds to the weight of proof that this was an intentional crime." He sighed and added in a low voice, for May's ears only, "I suspected it from the moment I saw this had taken place near this damned hotel, and that someone related to the hotel was the victim."

May knew that this confirmed all their worst suspicions.

Something like this could not have happened by chance. This crumpled bill must have been placed in his mouth by the killer. And that meant, without a doubt, that this was murder.

Sheriff Jack hurried over with an evidence bag, and Andy placed the bill carefully inside.

"We'll move the body now, and I'll take it in for examination," Andy said. "The postmortem should be completed by tomorrow at the latest."

"I hope it will provide more insight," Jack said. "The bill has been in the water for a long time, but there might be some forensic evidence to be found."

"I'll do my best," Andy promised.

"What do you think the five-dollar bill means?" Owen asked. He had taken off his scuba gear and was wearing blue jeans and a turtleneck top.

"I don't know what it means, but it confirms that we need to prioritize the investigation," Jack said.

The three of them stepped away, leaving the photographer to take pictures of the body. They moved into a huddle.

"Whoever put it there wanted us to find it. They wanted to send us a message," May said.

Andy's words had also reminded her that there was a huge amount of controversy surrounding this hotel. She glanced uneasily behind her, looking at its multistory facade. Was this a message about the hotel?

"Any guesses at what they're trying to say?" Owen asked, as if reading her mind.

May realized she had no idea. But she was suspicious, now, that the hotel was somehow providing the motive for this man's death. After all, this was the hotel's architect, murdered outside the hotel, in the area where the well-loved pier was due to be demolished. There could be different reasons, and she knew that Danny's private life must be examined closely, but for her the location of this crime was already a red flag.

"We need to look at every avenue and every motive, but we must keep in mind that there are a lot of people who didn't want this built," Jack said. It was clear to May that they were all thinking along the same lines.

"I hate to say it, but the hotel is already the subject of a lot of conflict," May said. "I know we've been getting so many complaints and so much negative feedback."

Jack nodded. "You don't know the half of it." He glanced at Owen.

"I've been handling the complaints," Owen said. "I've recorded every single one in writing, and graded them with red being the most serious, orange being more minor, and yellow still needing follow-up. And so far, they have filled a big file box."

"A lot of people are very angry about the project," Jack agreed.

"It's not just local people. People throughout Tamarack County have been making complaints," Owen said.

"So if the hotel was the reason for this crime, then we have a huge pool of potential suspects," May said. "This could be any one of a large number of people."

"That doesn't make it any easier," Jack said.

At that moment, they were interrupted by a shout from behind them.

"Hello there! Good morning!" a woman's voice called.

May turned to see a dark-haired woman approaching from the direction of the hotel. She was wearing a navy business suit and had her hair neatly tied back.

She was wearing high-heeled shoes that were sinking into the soft grass as she walked, slowing her down.

May hurried to meet her.

"I'm Jolene Barr, the hotel manager."

"Good morning, Ms. Barr," Owen said. He clearly recognized her, but didn't sound too pleased to see her.

"Hi, Deputy Lovell." She glared briefly in his direction before turning to May. "Some of my staff were saying there's a—a body here?" Her voice lowered and she glanced at the emergency vehicles.

"Deputy May Moore," May introduced herself. "Unfortunately, the victim is your hotel architect, Danny Charter."

Jolene's eyes widened. She looked horrified.

"Danny? Are you serious?" She glanced around. "That's his car there, isn't it? What happened? Did he drown, or—?"

"Unfortunately, we suspect that there was foul play and he was murdered," May said.

Jolene clapped her hands over her mouth.

"No! That's simply impossible!" she whispered.

"It's a tragic situation and we're hoping for more information to be available. We have a lot of questions that we will need answered," May advised her. "Perhaps you can give us some background? Did you know Danny well?"

"I—I—" Jolene seemed unable to say anything else. "This is just such a shock. I can't believe it. Danny—he's such a great guy. I knew him fairly well. I can try and give you some answers."

"How long had he been working on this project?" May asked, seeing out of the corner of her eye that Owen was taking notes as she spoke.

"He designed the initial hotel, of course, and I think he started working on the plans for the new wing in April," Jolene said. "He was the one who came up with the design, and he was the one who managed the construction. So he was very intensively involved. He lives out of state, in New York I think, and used to fly over regularly. He would stay at the hotel when he was doing his planning. I think he arrived here yesterday, just after lunch. I saw him in passing, and he said he was going to work on the plans, then go out for a meeting, and then spend time planning the site down by the lake."

"Who was the meeting with?" May asked.

She shook her head. "I've got no idea. Most likely with a supplier or a service provider. He sometimes used to go and view other buildings to see if different elements and designs would work for his builds."

"Who knew he would be here last night?" May asked.

Jolene shook her head. "I don't think any of us knew until he arrived. Like I said, he kept his own hours and consulted mostly with the hotel's owner, Bert Reed. I am sure he would have informed Mr. Reed that he was going to be here last night, but wouldn't have told any of us at this stage, especially since the build is still a few months away."

"Is Mr. Reed here today?" May asked.

"Mr. Reed is not here. I think he is in Minnesota, though, but he has interests in a number of different hotels and lodges. He could be at any of them."

"Does Danny have a family?" May asked, wanting a better picture.

"No, he's single. As far as I know."

"How did he get on with everyone in the hotel? Were there any conflicts? Any personal issues with any staff?"

Jolene shook her head. "I don't recall any fights or any conflicts. We're a happy family at Lakeside Heights. We strive to be a professional business. It's not our fault that the local people have been so aggressive and unpleasant," she added defensively.

Owen shifted from foot to foot as if he was longing to say something in response to this, but he didn't.

From the information she had so far, May thought this was looking less and less like a personal issue with Danny. He had no family, he was single, he didn't live in the area, and very few people knew he would have been here. So it was pointing more strongly in the direction of an aggrieved local who'd committed an impulsive crime when seeing the architect on the site of the proposed build. To her, anyway.

"Will this affect business in any way?" Jolene asked. "I mean, just so I'm aware. Will we be able to continue as normal? We have a couple of conferences booked."

May felt that question was a little glib, considering what had just happened. It seemed more like Jolene was thinking about business, and not the fact that her colleague had just been murdered.

Still, it wasn't May's place to criticize and Jolene was, after all, the hotel manager.

"You should be able to open and continue business as normal. But this area is a crime scene, so please don't allow guests to walk down this way."

"Of course. Of course," Jolene said. "It's a relief to hear we can go about our business."

She handed May one of her cards, and then turned and teetered up the grass, almost losing her fancy shoes with every step.

"Do you know her?" May asked.

Owen nodded. "She was my go-to person for all the hotel's complaints. Just as the residents complained nonstop, the hotel did, too. She used to harass me daily, and tell me they were being threatened and abused by the locals. It was honestly the equivalent of wasting police time."

May shook her head. This hotel was clearly a problem from start to finish, and it was solidifying her theory of how this murder might have occurred.

"If so few people knew Danny was here, and he had no obvious conflict with anyone, I don't think the hotel staff need to be our first priority. Before we start asking around at the hotel, I'd like to see your complaints file. There might well be some local people who we need to rule out as suspects initially. Let's see what's there, and decide if anyone stands out as having a strong motive."

CHAPTER FOUR

May and Owen arrived back at the Fairshore police department just a few minutes later. They parked outside and rushed inside. May felt very eager to learn the extent of these complaints. She needed to get a picture, not only of who was angriest, but also if anyone knew, or blamed, the architect personally.

They would also need to look into Danny's personal life, of course, but given that Danny was single, and that he lived out of state, and that this had happened while he was working on the hotel premises, and given the amount of bad blood that locals had, she felt this was the most important first step.

"Here is the file. It hasn't been easy, because I've had to work on this during the time when you've been doing courtroom security duty and managing the county jails."

May nodded. That had taken a few hours, most days, working together with Sheriff Jack who was teaching her the ropes. She'd always wonder why Owen had seemed stressed when they'd headed out on patrol again.

Owen lifted the file, with some difficulty, off the shelf.

May stared at it. It was enormous! It looked as if almost everyone in Tamarack County had, at some stage, put pen to paper or fingers to keyboards, to let the police know what they thought of this unwanted hotel. And she saw that the hotel had also lodged numerous complaints with the police. How was that all working out? May wondered.

"It looks like a lot," Owen agreed. "But many of them are from the same people. The red threats are in the front. They're the most serious ones. You'll see that people often complained directly to us, but they also threatened the hotel, and they then forwarded the complaints to us. The hotel did that all the time. Jolene got hold of my cell phone number and used to call and message me up to ten times a day. I did my best to help manage the situation, but there's only so much we can do."

"What did you do?"

Owen sighed. "I followed up on as many as possible. I issued warnings where complaints were regarded as threats, and visited residents, and also tried to liaise with the town planners regarding the complaints. The hotel got very nasty when it came to issues like noise and bad driving and dumping on their side. I was threatened with their lawyers a few times. They were definitely not working with the community, or prepared to resolve their own infractions."

"That so?" May asked, frowning.

"I have another entire file showing what I've done and who I've seen. But I admit, I haven't spoken to everyone. I tried to get through the red list at least, but there would often be more than twenty complaints in a day. But the interesting thing is that in the past couple of weeks, the complaints have reduced, and there haven't been nearly as many."

May quickly flipped to the red ones and started to read. Most of them were a variation on the same theme.

"I hate that hotel! It's creating noise pollution!"

"I wish that hotel would fall down!"

"I am personally going to drive my truck into that hotel, because of all the traffic it's creating."

"The hotel is ruining the environment of this area. Someone should set fire to it."

"I don't want to see any buildings other than trees here."

"The architect, Danny Charter, is nothing more than a criminal, and he should be shot for having gone ahead without all the right approvals in place."

May thought that last comment was very interesting.

"Owen," she said, "can you do a search through the complaints to see if anyone else has named the architect in their complaint? That's the only one I've read so far that's named him personally."

"Yes, it's the only one that I remember, too. The others were more general. It was all about 'the hotel' and no single individual."

That represented a clear starting point to May.

The complaint to the police that the architect should be shot was from a local man named Freddy Featherstone, who lived a few miles north of Chestnut Hill.

The hotel had sent in complaints about Freddy, too. He'd called them at least once a day. He'd written emails. Demanded to know who the "key players" were and had then contacted them directly too.

And so the war had escalated.

"I have met with Freddy Featherstone twice so far and issued him an official police warning. And I even offered to meet with him and Jolene and try to mediate the situation, but they both said they were too busy," Owen explained.

May shook her head.

"It sounds as if you did everything you could. There was clearly no desire on either of their sides to actually resolve this." Until now, she thought.

"I guess we need to go and question Freddy again now," Owen said. "I wonder if he'll behave differently this time. He was very aggressive the previous times, just so you know."

"That's good to know. Let's see if there's any difference in his attitude now."

*

It was the first time that May had been to Freddy Featherstone's premises, although Owen drove the route with the ease of previous familiarity. She had visited Chestnut Hill many times, and they'd been called out to a few of the surrounding lodges and campsites for minor crimes, but so far this one had been off her radar.

"He's a fisherman," Owen explained, as they headed onto the main road circling the lake. "A professional fisherman, I mean. He fishes for bass. He runs a campsite where people can vacation."

"Really?" May asked.

"Yes. He has a campground. He's been doing it for the past ten years and he's built up a loyal following of clients."

"So why has he been angry about the hotel?"

"Because he says they are deliberately trying to make him go under," Owen said.

"How's that?" May asked.

"He said the hotel bought up a few surrounding businesses— restaurants, stores, and so on—and then deliberately closed them down to starve him out and drive business away from his area. They want to position themselves as a destination for fishermen and build some upmarket chalets."

"Doing that seems like a very underhanded move," May observed. "Is it true?"

"I don't think it's altogether true, but it might be partly true," Owen said.

He turned off the main road.

"Here we are," he said.

There was a small stream running through the grounds, with a bridge across it, leading to a large wooden sign that read *Featherstone Campground—Enjoy Fishing and Boating*, with a rainbow trout on it.

A little shop stood at the entrance. Through its wide window, May saw fishing rods hanging from the wall, and a variety of different bait and lures displayed.

Beyond the store, May could see a few different campsites within the spacious grounds. The area was green, treed and shady.

"This looks like a nice spot," May said. "It doesn't deserve to go under. It's not even that close to the hotel."

She stepped out of the vehicle and gazed around.

It seemed a pity that anyone would want to try and destroy it. Why would a large hotel target a smaller business like this? Had they even done so?

May hoped they could get clear answers.

She and Owen walked across the bridge and headed to the wooden kiosk on their right. There, an attendant smiled warmly.

"We're looking for Freddy," May said. "It's in connection with an investigation."

"Ah. He's moved out of his house. He unfortunately had to sell off that piece of land."

"Is that so?" May asked. This was sounding worrying.

"He's now living in the communal camping area. That's his yurt."

"It is?" May looked in the direction the attendant was pointing. "Is he inside?"

Amid the scattering of colorful tents she saw a plain brown yurt near the center of the campground.

"I'm not sure where he is," the attendant explained.

"What does Freddy look like?" May murmured to Owen as they headed across the grass.

"He's tall and blond, with a mustache and a ponytail," Owen muttered back.

There was a fair amount of activity in the campsite as they approached. Kids were running around, screaming and yelling, climbing trees and playing in the shallow ponds. People were arriving with picnic baskets and setting up tents and walking dogs.

May had no idea where to start looking.

She turned back to the attendant, but saw he was on his cell phone, speaking urgently.

It suddenly occurred to May that he might be warning Freddy that the police had arrived.

"I'm worried about this," she said to Owen. "We need to find this man fast, because if he's guilty, I think the campsite attendant has given him the heads-up that we're here."

"He could well have done that," Owen said. "I think we need to shut down this campground and get the attendant to close up the gates, and then do a proper search."

"Let's go back and do that," May said.

But as she was about to turn back, she narrowed her eyes. "Is that smoke coming out of the top of the yurt?"

"Smoke?" Owen sounded startled. "So it is. What's going on?"

As she watched, the smoke thickened. It coiled up, first gray and then black.

This was an emergency, May realized. Something had gone terribly wrong.

"Freddy's yurt's on fire!"

May and Owen sprinted across the campground in the direction of the now-blazing yurt.

CHAPTER FIVE

"Mr. Featherstone!" May yelled, sprinting across the campsite. Now there were concerned shouts and cries. Side by side, she and Owen raced toward the yurt. The crackling and roar of the fire grew louder.

Alerted by the smoke, people were racing toward the yurt from all directions. Apart from one person, May suddenly noticed. A tall man in a black baseball cap was racing away, heading down the hill.

May grabbed Owen's arm.

"Is that him? Is that Freddy?" she asked.

Owen nodded.

"That's him!"

Too late, May realized what the ulterior motive for the fire had been.

The fire had been designed to draw all the attention, while Freddy himself fled the campground.

"Don't let him get away!" she shouted.

She and Owen turned, now running away from the blazing yurt, and sprinted in Freddy's direction. The tall, blond man in the baseball cap turned and saw them coming.

Quickly he began to run, weaving through the tents and trees, setting a fast pace as he fled downhill.

"Stop!" Owen yelled.

Owen took off after the man, with May right behind him.

"Stop!" she cried at the top of her voice. But she didn't think he was listening at all.

They were heading toward the road. A small group of people had gathered there to watch the fire. They gasped and pointed as they saw the burning yurt, and the chase.

Freddy glanced over his shoulder. He clearly saw May and Owen in pursuit.

"Stop!" May yelled again, but instead, Freddy ran faster. He sprinted up to the edge of the camping ground.

Then he jumped the fence.

In front of her, Owen placed his hands on the top and vaulted nimbly over.

May grabbed it, determined not to let this barrier slow her down. She lifted herself as high as she could and then jumped over, staggering as she landed but then charging ahead.

Freddy was heading for the lake, she saw. He raced to the water's edge, where he speedily untied a small rowboat.

With a powerful and practiced technique, the blond man began rowing away from the shore.

Drawing the oars back, he took long and powerful strokes. The boat was quickly slipping away.

Why was he running away? Where was he going?

"We need to swim after him!" Owen said, breathing hard as he gazed at the departing rowboat.

"Wait! Let's think this through," May gasped. "If we think intelligently, we can outmaneuver him."

She looked around.

Fifty yards away, by the pier, a small speedboat had just arrived back from a sail. The owner was climbing out and preparing to moor it.

"Let's borrow that!" May decided. "It's our only chance to catch up. Swimming isn't going to cut it."

They raced for the speedboat. May felt a sense of urgency as they pounded up to it. Freddy was rowing hard, and had a big head start. There were several treed islands in this area of the lake that would provide cover if he could get past them. They had only a minute or two before he rowed out of sight and vanished into the vastness of the lake.

"Do you mind if we use your boat for a minute?" she asked, breathlessly.

He stared at her in surprise. "Why don't you go and rent your own?" he asked.

"I'm the police," she added, showing him her badge. "We need to catch up with a suspect."

"The police?" He looked astonished and apologetic. "Er—sure. Sure."

Quickly, he climbed out of the boat, and May and Owen jumped in.

The figure in the rowboat was rowing faster than before, desperate to get away.

Owen grabbed the tiller. "Let's go catch him," he said.

The motor roared as Owen turned the throttle. The boat sped away, bouncing over the waves. The rowboat was growing ever smaller in the distance. But now the speedboat was gaining. May stared at it, willing the speedboat to go faster.

Freddy knew how to row, May realized. And he was rowing for his life.

As they neared him, the rowboat veered off to the left.

"Where's he going?" May asked. "Is he trying to lose us?"

"No," Owen said. "He's trying to reach land. That's what he's doing, and it's not going to be good for us."

The rowboat was heading for a strip of beach. Freddy Featherstone was going to try and escape into the woods. If he got to shore, she feared they would lose him.

"Go, Owen! Faster!" May implored. This was going to be touch and go.

They caught up just before the shore. Owen steered the speedboat expertly up next to the rowboat.

"Go away!" Freddy yelled at them. He was still rowing frantically, but as May leaned over she managed to grab one of the flying oars. It almost slipped out of her hand, and then she nearly fell out of the motorboat. Owen grasped her other arm just in time.

Leaning further forward, May managed to grasp the mooring rope. Breathing hard, she scrambled back into her boat, holding it firmly.

They had him tethered to their own boat, and now he couldn't get away.

Freddy looked up at Owen, his eyes wide and frightened. His face was covered in sweat, and he was breathing hard.

"I am not the guilty party here, Deputy Lovell!" he gasped. "You've got to let me go!"

Before May could stop him, Freddy jerked the oars, trying to free himself.

The speedboat rocked wildly, almost tipping over.

"Don't," May warned. "Or the boat might capsize."

Freddy abandoned his struggles with an angry sigh.

"Are you also from the police?" he asked May. "What did I do?"

"I'm Deputy May Moore," she said. "You need to come with us, because we have to question you regarding a serious crime."

Freddy shook his head. His eyes were fearful.

"No. You can't do this to me! You can't!" He looked around wildly. "Please, I didn't do anything! You can't take me in! I'm innocent! I never meant to cause any trouble."

From the way he'd reacted, May was far from convinced of that.

"We'll decide that when we have had the chance to question you properly," May told him sternly. "For now, you don't have a choice.

You attempted to flee the police, and if you don't want to face criminal charges, then come with us quietly. No more trying to run!"

*

Thirty minutes later, Freddy was perched uneasily on a chair in the interrogation room of the Fairshore police precinct.

It was a small room, more of a spare office than an official interrogation room, but it had been fitted out with an observation window, and there was a tape recorder on the desk.

May walked in and stared hard at Freddy.

"Mr. Featherstone, you committed an act of arson in the campground. And then you fled from police," she said. "I'm in possession of numerous complaints you have made, and which have been made against you, regarding the hotel. You have been calling, emailing, threatening. You named the architect in your threats."

Freddy stared at her nervously.

"Did the hotel send you to me? I know they sent you! They want to arrest me."

"This isn't just about the hotel," May said. "We are investigating a murder, and you are a potential suspect. If you are innocent, then there is nothing to worry about. But if you are guilty, then we need to know that as quickly as possible."

"A murder? No way! What murder?" Freddy now sounded appalled.

"The murder of Danny Charter, the hotel's architect," May said firmly.

Danny's mouth dropped open.

"Serious?" he said incredulously. "That man's dead?"

"Yes. And from the messages you sent, you have a strong motive," May said sternly. "Why did you run when we arrived at the campsite?"

"I—I thought the hotel was sending you to cause trouble! I don't trust them. They want to destroy me because I'm standing up for the community."

"You knew about the murder?"

"I had no idea! If I had known, I wouldn't have run, because I would have known it would make me look guilty! I know there were issues between us. I could see that architect was breaking all the rules. I know he was cutting corners. I read up on the local by-laws when I was building our campsite amenities. So I had a personal problem with him,

I admit. I felt like I was speaking out for everyone. But to do something like that? I wouldn't!"

"Where were you last night?"

"I wasn't even in town last night. I was at a fishing competition in Maine. I flew there yesterday morning, stayed overnight, and got back early this morning."

May glanced at Owen.

"Do you have proof of that?" Owen asked.

"Sure, of course I do!"

"Can you show us?"

He lifted a finger. "Before I go any further, I want my lawyer. I still don't trust this hotel. So I'll show you the proof of flights, but if you have any other questions, I'd like my lawyer to be present."

"Show me," May said.

The man opened his phone. A moment later, May was looking at the confirmation of the competition entry, the flight booking, and even the online boarding pass.

Sure enough, he had definitely, and legitimately, been out of town yesterday.

"For now, that's all we need from you. And you are free to go," she said reluctantly.

He got up looking self-satisfied.

May felt deeply frustrated. This had been a waste of time. This man had by far the strongest motive. He'd made the most serious threats, had named the architect, and had harassed the hotel. There was clearly bad blood between them.

But he hadn't been in town at the time of the murder.

However, as Freddy stalked out, he turned and said something else. Something that May hadn't expected at all.

"If you look at my emails to that hotel, you'll see that I stopped bothering them two or three weeks ago now. That's when I read the article online saying that they will never be financially viable, and that they're doomed to failure. That's when I realized all I have to do is sit tight and wait for them to go under, and then my little campsite will be stronger than ever. I believe in karma. The big wheel turns," he concluded dramatically.

He brushed past her and headed out the door.

May exchanged a curious glance with Owen.

Doomed to failure?

"Let's find that article now and see what it says," she decided.

CHAPTER SIX

As soon as Featherstone had left, May got online and went hunting.

"Remember, I mentioned the complaints tailed off in the past couple of weeks," Owen said, paging through the folder as she searched. "I wonder if this is the reason why. It seems like a lot of people must have read that article."

"Here it is," May said. "This is the one. Look, it's in the financial section of the *Tamarack News*."

Unfortunately, she seldom read that section. Usually, the community news was more relevant to her job.

She was astonished to see the headline.

"The Lakeside Heights: A Doomed Project."

"What does it say?" Owen asked.

"Here's the introduction," May read out. "*The big, beautiful new hotel... and the total financial failure it represents. The story behind the property that is doomed to failure. Read on to find out why.*"

"Wow. That's very hard hitting," Owen agreed. "Go on. What else does it say?"

"*The problem with the Lakeside Heights project is that it's not viable,*" May continued. "*They've bought up a load of land in a remote location, and they are building a huge and spectacular hotel there. Everyone who has been to the site so far has been impressed with the hotel—but what the company hasn't told investors is that the hotel, when it opens, will only make a profit if the entire resort is crowded with guests 24/7. And in this sparsely populated part of the world, that's not possible. The hotel miscalculated badly. With plans afoot to build a second wing, they need to go back to the drawing board and be aware of who their customers are.*"

She glanced at Owen, knowing that his background was in accounting.

"That sounds like a knowledgeable piece," he said. "If they've overcapitalized, that's a very serious error and they are going to suffer for it down the line."

"*The hotel has potential in terms of the site, but it is being developed too fast and too broadly for the local market to be capable of carrying it*," May read. "*A second wing will only compound the disaster.*"

Owen raised his eyebrows.

"But the company doesn't seem to be aware of this fact," May said. "From what I've seen, they're still planning to go ahead."

"Until they discover that they can't turn a profit," Owen said. "If they are still in denial, they are going to be in trouble. Many businesses have hit the rocks as a result of not understanding their market."

"There's more here," May said. "*In this remote area, it's essential to know who your market is, and also to cooperate with the locals*," May read. "*It's not just about business. The company has not cooperated with locals. Financially, in their quest for domination of the market, they have bought up a lot of the surrounding land, and this in turn has driven up the price of land in the area, and that has made it more expensive for everyone else. In fact, the tax base is going to be damaged by this project.*"

"That's true," Owen said. "That's not how business should be done."

"Can you hunt for anything more specific about their financial dealings?"

"I can try," Owen said. "But if they are still working on the hotel, they must be confident of finding the money to finish it."

Perhaps we should speak to the journalist?" May asked.

Owen nodded. "I see here it's written by the financial expert Emily Oxman. Let's have a word with Emily. There might also be information she didn't, or couldn't, write."

May dialed the number of the *Tamarack News*.

"Hi, I'm from Fairshore police, and I need to speak with Emily Oxman. It's urgent," she said as soon as she got through.

She waited while they put her through. A moment later, someone picked up.

"This is Adele Wong, the financial editor," a woman said.

"Ms. Wong, we're looking to speak to the journalist who wrote the article about the Lakeside Heights," May said.

"She's not in. She's out researching a story. But I managed and edited the article, so maybe I can help," Adele said.

"This is about a murder investigation," May said. "We're investigating the death of Danny Charter. He was the architect in charge of the hotel project, and he was murdered last night."

"Good heavens! Murdered?" Adele sounded shocked.

"I'm hoping that we can get some background information on the project. We're wondering if this bleak financial outlook might somehow be related to what has happened. Is there any more information you could give us? Did you get any more information from the company? Or from other sources?"

"I was the one who first researched the hotel, and then handed the article to the journalist to write. So I can definitely help," Adele said.

"Please explain," May said.

"I started out looking into the land purchase, but as I looked into it, I got more and more concerned about the finances. I realized that this company had taken on a huge amount of debt to build the hotel and start the development. And that they were planning to take on some more. What that means is that this is a highly speculative investment. It's a huge gamble. Every hotel comes with huge costs. Mostly in terms of staffing, especially for a high-end establishment. You have cleaning, housekeeping, maintenance, porterage, reception, waitressing. Never mind the initial build, I just don't understand how they will cover those. Labor costs are the biggest expense to any hotel, and I think at the moment, those represent more than forty percent of the total costs."

"That's significant," May agreed.

"So, therefore, I concluded that unless the hotel is completely full all the time, it won't make a profit. And that is unlikely to happen."

May thought for a moment. "What else did you find out?"

"There is usually a risk assessment report done before a project like this is approved. I was able to get hold of a copy of that report. As far as they can tell, they can't foresee any risk large enough to prevent them making a profit. But, as far as I'm concerned, that's just wishful thinking. The fact is, they have not done their homework. They have not done enough market research, and they have no idea how many guests they can expect to have or what revenue they can expect."

"Did you speak to the hotel at all?"

"The CEO was not available when I called and did not get back to me by deadline, or present his side. So their comment was simply 'no comment.' Of course, he called me angrily as soon as he read the article," Adele said.

"And what did he say then?"

"Apart from threatening to sue the *Tamarack News* as well as Emily in her capacity as journalist, he said that there is no way the hotel will fail and that we had our facts completely wrong. He said that the community was sabotaging the hotel but that once they realized its success, they would have to stop and he'd demand an apology. He also said they had insurance in place for the second wing, so that no matter what happened, they would be covered. The insurance kicks in if the build is delayed or sabotaged or put on hold due to unforeseen events."

"Is that so?" May asked, her ears pricking up at this.

"Yes. I found him very arrogant. I told him insurance can't pay for the ongoing operational costs and he then told me to go to hell. He wanted me to print an apology but I refused, as he hadn't complied with the request for information in the first place, and we stood by our research."

"Thank you so much for this information," May said.

She ended the call, feeling excited.

Owen had clearly also picked up on the most important piece of information, and the one that would get them on the next step.

"We need to find out the details of this insurance policy," Owen said.

May nodded. "It sounds like that could be a game changer in terms of who might have committed the murder. After all, having an architect tragically dead on site would certainly be an unforeseen delay. And it might allow the CEO of a failing hotel to cash in on something he'd realized might not be as lucrative as he'd hoped."

"I'll contact the hotel and ask how I can get hold of him," Owen said. "I remember his name. Bert Reed. And they said he was in Minnesota. We need to speak to Mr. Reed and find out exactly how he stood to benefit."

CHAPTER SEVEN

May was hoping that they could head straight out and confront Bert Reed. But as Owen made call after call, she realized it wasn't going to be so easy.

"Nobody seems to know where he is," Owen said, putting down the phone after the third call. "I literally don't believe this. Not even the hotel manager knows. Or at any rate, she says she doesn't know."

"How can they not know where the owner is?" May asked, incredulous. Surely he had to be available and in the area, given that his architect had just been murdered? Why wasn't he at the Lakeside Heights sorting things out?

"He's definitely in the state. Everyone agrees on that. But he seems to own a massive amount of property. He owns several other hotels and he often stays in hotels he's thinking of buying, also, Jolene said."

"He definitely does seem to be very wealthy," May said. "Can't they give you his phone number?"

Owen sighed. "I got a number. I have no idea if it's his number. But it's turned off."

"I would guess if his phone is off at this time, he's either in an urgent meeting or he's playing golf," May decided. For some reason, she thought this man sounded like the type of person who would play golf in a crisis. "Just on a flyer, perhaps it would be worth calling the hotels within, say, a fifty-mile radius of here that are five-star and have golf courses. It might narrow the field."

"Good idea," Owen said.

"In the meantime, I'll—"

At that exact moment May's phone rang.

To her astonishment, it was her older sister, Kerry. This case had brought Kerry to top of mind. May had been thinking of her and now she was calling, as if the thoughts had summoned her.

But Kerry hardly ever called her. What was happening?

Mystified, she picked up.

"Hello, May." Her sister's voice, loud and confident, rang down the line, and May couldn't prevent a cold shiver at the sound.

This was Kerry. Self-assured. Successful. Knowing that life would fall in with her ideas and that she'd end up on top.

"Hi, Kerry," May said.

She had not heard from her sister since Kerry had gone to the East Coast when the FBI had been called in to solve a serial crime.

"You won't believe this," Kerry said. She sounded as if she was laughing.

That was right, May decided. Whatever her sister was going to say, May probably wouldn't believe it.

"I've arrived at your airport—the local one—and there are no rental cars to be had! None! I mean, I think they had, like, two in total, and both the tourists visiting Tamarack County already using them!" She laughed, as if this was a really funny joke.

"Wait, what?" May spluttered. Her sister? Was here?

This was a bombshell. She'd had no idea she was visiting.

Or was she somehow involved in this investigation? she wondered with a twist of her stomach. Had the FBI stepped in at the hotel's request?

Surely not, May thought, forcing herself to think logically. She couldn't possibly be here for work, and this hadn't sounded like a work-related reason either.

May knew only too well that sharp, brisk, businesslike tone her sister adopted when dealing with work matters. And it wasn't in her voice now.

"I've come to visit the folks," Kerry clarified. "And I don't want to ask them to come out and fetch me because it's a sort of a surprise."

May saw where this was going.

"You want me to pick you up?"

"If you have time."

May didn't have time. She was busy with a murder case.

"Time? To take you to the folks? No, I don't," she said, hearing the note of panic in her own voice. "Now? Can't you call a cab?"

Kerry sighed.

"Okay. There's a reason why I need you to drive me there. There's a big surprise. I have news."

"What news is that?"

"I'll tell you when I see you. And I want you to be there when I tell them. It won't take long!"

And the airport drive there and back? That would be still more time. May agonized, feeling torn by the demands of her job versus family loyalty.

"Go," Owen hissed at her in a stage whisper, waving his arms, clearly picking up on the dilemma she was in. "Don't stress. I'm busy researching the CEO!"

"I'm on my way," she snapped to her sister, wondering how Kerry always managed to get her way. Ending the call, she looked gratefully at Owen.

"Who knows what this is about? But I'll be back in less than an hour," she said.

She grabbed her keys and purse and was out the door.

As she drove, May wished she could have felt just a little bit more excited at seeing her sister again. But Kerry always had a strange effect on her. She was always so sure of herself and of what she wanted. She was her parents' favorite, their golden child and their icon of success.

Plus, Kerry had aced the FBI entrance exams and gotten into the academy, and today she was an FBI agent working in the Behavioral Analysis Unit.

May had recently been promoted to Tamarack County deputy, the first female deputy and the youngest ever county deputy, but she knew that her achievements were small-time compared to Kerry's swathe of success.

May never felt good enough, or smart enough, or even good-looking enough when Kerry was around. May had always struggled to be taken seriously in comparison to her sister. She always felt small-time. Small-town and small-time, compared to her sister who had made it big. Nothing she did ever seemed to compare. Even solving the community's recent serial killer case seemed like a minor accomplishment, since Kerry caught serial killers who were terrorizing entire cities or states.

She'd gotten used to it. She'd even managed to have a sense of humor about it, most times anyway. But right now, she had to get through the next few minutes. Because Kerry had told her there was news to come.

She pulled up in the pick-up zone where Kerry was waiting. She cut a sophisticated figure with her short blond hair, her wide blue eyes, her flawless skin, and her lean, athletic figure. She was wearing blue jeans and a taupe leather jacket, fabulous-looking ankle-length boots in soft brown leather, and expensive-looking sunglasses that accentuated her high cheekbones.

"Hi, sis," she said, as she climbed into the car, stowing her carry-on in the back seat. "I'm so happy you could come and get me. I literally can't believe this place. No rental cars available? I mean, really?"

"No problem," May said, offering a smile that she hoped was warm and friendly. "It's nice to see you. But why are you here?"

"I have some news!" Kerry grinned at her.

"What news?"

"I'm engaged!"

May nearly drove off the road as Kerry stuck her left hand in front of her, showing off a massive diamond ring which somehow, amid everything else she'd taken in about her sister, May hadn't noticed.

May stared at the ring, feeling awestruck and also, for a moment, horribly jealous.

Everything in Kerry's life kept going right! What May wouldn't give to have a decent, steady boyfriend whom she loved and who loved her back!

But then her pang of jealousy was swept aside by genuine happiness for her sister.

"That's amazing. Congratulations," she said.

"It happened on our European getaway. We got back yesterday from a whirlwind weekend trip to Venice." Kerry was beaming. "Brandon and I have been dating for a year. He's one of the country's top business lawyers. You know, he's been all over the news recently for his work on the economic bailout. He is amazing and I'm so lucky to have him."

"Wow," May said. "I mean, wow. I'm so happy for you both. I know Mom and Dad will be thrilled too."

"Well, of course. Mom was asking me last time I was here if I thought it was serious with him. But we've both been so busy that even something this important ended up taking a back seat. Anyway, this past weekend, we flew to Venice. It was supposed to be a quick vacation, but he proposed there. It was just unbelievably romantic, and a total surprise to me. On a gondola under the Bridge of Sighs!"

To Venice?

May dreamed of going to Venice. And Kerry had been! Not just been, but been and proposed to. May could never match that level of romance.

She'd been married for a few years at the age of twenty-one. Strangely enough, her ex was also a lawyer, though more of the ambulance-chaser type than the high flyer who'd fallen for Kerry.

It hadn't worked out and here she was, divorced, with no new love on the horizon.

"Anyway," Kerry said. "I know you're probably very busy. Early summer in town must mean a lot of drunken students and the like for the police to manage. But I'm glad you were able to give me a ride here, and at least you know now!"

"I'm so thrilled for you," May said, turning into her parents' driveway and parking on the gravel. She decided not to tell Kerry about the murder case. Most likely, she wouldn't listen anyway.

May climbed out. Alerted by the sound of her car, her father was already at the door.

"May, my angel! I always hear you from a mile away. Did you have a chance to get that exhaust pipe looked at? I think it might need some attention."

And then Kerry climbed out and May watched, feeling small, as her father's face lit up.

"Honey!" he called back into the house. "Kerry's here!"

"Kerry?" May heard her mother's cry from the kitchen.

A moment later, she rushed out.

"Kerry, my precious girl, I'm so glad you're here," she said, hugging her oldest child. "What an amazing surprise! You didn't tell us you were coming!"

"Mom," Kerry said, sounding pleased. "I have some big news to share."

"What is it?" Her mother's eyes were shining. Glancing at them, May saw how alike they were. Most definitely, Kerry had inherited more of her mother's slim, blond, beautiful looks. And her perfectionist streak. No wonder she was the favorite daughter.

"I'm engaged!" Kerry lifted her left hand, the diamond sparkling in the rays of the midday sun.

"Oh, what happy news," her mother said, and May saw tears in her eyes. "You must be on cloud nine. Brandon is such a wonderful man!"

"I sure am," Kerry said. Her elation was obvious.

Her mother's focus was stuck on her oldest daughter. Kerry glowed with delight and her mother was the perfect audience for it.

May felt a stab of envy.

Kerry was the golden child. Kerry was never going to have to struggle as hard as she did. She'd never have to feel like a failure.

"Girls, can you come in for a moment?" her father said. "I want to hear all about this."

"May, it's so good to see you," her mother said, turning to her at last and looking slightly guilty at having forgotten all about her younger daughter. "Did you know about Kerry's surprise?"

"Not a thing." May smiled. It already felt forced.

"Is Brandon going to come out here as well?" Her mother turned back to Kerry.

"Yes. He's just wrapping up a big case he's working on. As soon as that's done, he's going to fly out. I'm waiting on his phone call to find out when it will be."

"And how's your work going? Do you have any interesting cases on the go?"

"Yes, we've just wrapped up a fascinating case. It's a killer who struck at five-year intervals. I actually worked out his identity by going back into the archives and analyzing the behavior of everyone close to his victims."

"How amazing! You know, we are also busy with a very disturbing case," May tried, but she could see her parents didn't even notice.

"Going back into the archives!" her mother echoed.

May sighed inwardly. How she wished the conversation would flow two ways, and that she could talk about her work, too, and contribute to the dialogue.

But Kerry's news and Kerry's work had eclipsed it. Her parents were too busy cooing over Kerry to pay any attention to her.

She looked at her watch.

"Speaking of work, I have to get going. I took time off to pick Kerry up."

"You can't stay and chat with us?"

"I'm sorry," she said, feeling like a disappointing child again. "I'd love to another time."

"Well, let's organize a get-together. I understand work can't wait," her mother said.

At that moment, her father asked, "Hey, May, do you know anything about that local death? I heard something about it on the local WhatsApp group earlier. They weren't sure if it was a drowning or a murder. Is it even true? I guess if it is a murder, it'll go to the FBI?"

"Yes, it is true. We're handling it."

May felt like this question was too little, too late. And they hadn't yet made any progress on the case, so there was really nothing more to say. She could see Kerry's curious glance, but ignored it. Instead, she turned and walked back to the car, feeling heavy hearted.

As she got there, her phone rang.

It was Owen, and seeing his number, her heart lifted. Perhaps this meant there was progress, she thought.

Owen sounded excited when she picked up.

"I've found out where Bert Reed is staying," he said. "Your idea about the golf courses worked out! He's at a golf resort he owns about twenty miles from here."

May felt her heart leap. She was able to derail her thoughts away from the frustrating topic of family and focus on the demands of their case.

"I'll be back in five minutes. Let's head straight out together," she said.

CHAPTER EIGHT

The killer watched the window through narrowed eyes.

The target was inside, strolling around the luxury lodge. A woman, wearing an expensive designer dress in sumptuous satin fabric, speaking on the phone.

She was flawlessly made up. The cosmetics concealed the sour, arrogant set to her mouth. But the killer could see it. Her eyes had a cold look in them, a hard gaze.

In the stillness of the air, the killer could even hear the words she was saying.

"I have to go," she said into the phone. "There are deals to be made. They won't wait. Yes, I can make eight p.m. That will be fine. Look, I'm not handling that side so much anymore. I'm staying out of it for a while. I'll give you the number of the person you need to speak to."

And then she hung up the phone.

She turned, looking out the window, and the killer shrank back, because it was taking a big chance to be here now, watching her, although it was necessary for the job that needed to be done. That had to be done.

But as the killer had suspected, this woman was too arrogant to believe she was in any danger. She probably saw herself in the tinted glass and nothing more.

She turned, looked in the mirror, and then took off her pearl earrings.

As she paced about the room, the killer felt a rush of pure loathing for her. In the killer's mind, the targets were all despicable.

And this target was the lowest of the low.

She was a woman who thought of no-one but herself, who lived in a fantasy world of her own making. But within that world, she was evil and corrupt and deserved to die.

The killer retreated, watching, waiting. The timing needed to be perfect, and it wasn't yet.

With her phone call concluded, the woman turned up the music. It wasn't music the killer liked. This woman had poor taste. The ugly sounds throbbed and pulsed loudly, contaminating the peaceful air. The woman smiled, her mouth twisting. She liked this hellish beat.

And so did the killer, but only because it would muffle the noise that was needed for the scene to be set.

The woman took out her phone again and looked at it.

"I'm waiting," she said out loud, as if she were expecting a message or an update.

But then she tossed the phone on the bed, and the killer saw she didn't really care. She turned the music up even louder. A powerful beat and a screeching voice, like something that would come out of a monster's throat.

Then she moved to her jewelry box, selecting different earrings from the massive display.

There was nothing but the sound of the music, heavy and ugly, throbbing. The killer felt another spurt of rage, because this woman was a monster.

It was time.

Nerves of steel would be needed for this next step.

The killer moved to the patio door. Pulled the handle down. It opened, because the lock had been blocked earlier with a folded piece of paper that the killer now took.

It was a five-dollar bill.

The killer opened the door, entered the room, closed the door, and then moved quickly and quietly to the bathroom, because that was the place needed for the conclusion to this revenge.

In this luxury lodge there was a giant, oval tub. It would be perfect, the killer thought. And with this deafening music blaring, the woman would not hear the tub filling up.

The killer twisted the knob, and cold water gushed out of the faucet, filling the tub. The tub filled up quickly. The water supply in this place was generous and powerful. That was what the rich expected, of course.

The killer moved to the door of the bathroom. Waited. The time had to be right, but that time was approaching, and very soon, it would be the moment to make the kill.

And in the quietness of the pristine white room, the killer could see, quite easily, the target's reflection in the mirror. That smug, self-satisfied expression that made the killer's blood boil with rage.

She was a cold, narcissistic person who had absolutely no empathy. She destroyed people and didn't care. That was who she was. It was who they all were. Every one of the targets was the same.

It was too much for the killer.

The water in the tub began to spill over the edge, and a puddle formed on the floor.

It was time.

The killer crept to the bathroom door. This was the most risky part, moving through to the bedroom to actually approach this appalling woman. It needed to be done smoothly, confidently, and fast. Hesitation would mean failure. Resolve would mean success.

The woman was still preening in front of the mirror, carefully choosing a necklace that matched the earrings. Sifting through her ridiculous, overpriced baubles was all that mattered in her empty life.

Her appearance, her status, her self-importance were the only qualities that defined her, the killer thought.

And then, at last, she turned away from the mirror and went to her wardrobe. She opened it and took out an expensive handbag.

She opened it up and packed a few items inside. Lipstick, Kleenex, cash. Trivial items that marked the meaninglessness of her life.

Her cold gaze turned to the mirror. She smiled. She was the center of her own world, and the killer could see that in the woman's eyes.

The woman's back was turned. She was standing in front of the window, looking out at the view, probably wondering when to go into the lobby to wait for her limousine to arrive. The killer crept inside, knowing that this was a critical time when everything could go wrong. If the woman turned, she would see an intruder, she would scream, and the element of surprise that was so badly needed would be totally destroyed.

But she didn't turn.

She was so arrogant that she had no fear that someone was behind her. After all, she had not heard the killer come in. She was so infatuated with herself, so obsessed with the possessions she'd accumulated. All she cared about was showing off her trinkets and flaunting her status, even though her entire identity and wealth were rooted in suffering and blood.

An electric thrill raced through the killer's body. This was the long-awaited moment, the time when the planning would be put to the test.

A weapon was needed. There was the perfect item. A quick detour to the fireplace to grab the poker. And then into the bedroom, moving fast now.

The woman looked up, finally sensing a presence. Too little, too late. Sorry for you, you deserved it, the killer thought, jumping forward to smash her over the head with the iron poker.

Her eyes rolled up into her head, and she slumped in the killer's arms. The killer dragged her out, ready for the next step—the final, killing step.

The music was blaring as if nothing had happened, as if the woman were still staring out at those expansive, private lawns.

A fireplace poker. A full bathtub. A five-dollar bill. It was payback time. The scene had been set and now the conclusion to this cruel, meaningless life would play out.

The killer's eyes were cold and hard. There was no mercy in them.

There was no mercy in the killer's heart either.

CHAPTER NINE

May sat in the passenger seat of Owen's car as Owen turned off the main road and approached the marble-fronted facade of the Mount Amethyst five-star hotel and golf resort. The hotel was in an exquisitely beautiful, mountainous area that was about twenty miles out of Tamarack County.

"Bert Reed sure does stay in style," May said, as they drove down the paved driveway, lined with stone pillars twined with vines. "He owns this place?"

"Yes. From the research I've done, he's very wealthy. As in, extremely," Owen explained. "He owns about five different luxury hotels here in Minnesota, and a few others in New York State. Then he also has interests in a few other businesses, which from the description I think are probably strip clubs. So far, those are only in New York State."

"Interesting," May said, filing this away.

The resort itself was a fabulous building of white stone, with ornate columns. The whole complex was surrounded by verdant gardens and manicured lawns, and a golf course stretched beyond the perimeter of the building.

They parked in the main lot and got out. The car lot was filled with expensive vehicles: BMWs, Mercedes, Audis, and a Porsche. Valets in black and white uniforms were polishing the cars. Owen and May parked and walked up the stairway into the hotel lobby. It was a large, beautiful room, with a glass ceiling that let in the sunlight from above.

They headed to the reception desk—a massive marble console on the far side of this exquisite space.

"Good morning. Welcome to the Mount Amethyst Hotel and Golf Resort," the dark-haired receptionist said, smiling.

"Good morning." May showed her badge. "We understand Mr. Bert Reed is residing at your hotel. We'd like to speak to him."

Now the receptionist's warm smile disappeared and she looked taken aback.

"Mr. Reed? Is he expecting you? He's got back-to-back meetings here all day."

"No. It's in connection with a murder investigation. He'll know about the murder, as it involves his new hotel. But he's not aware we're here now."

"Oh! Let me call him."

The receptionist quickly dialed. She spoke in a low voice, paused, listened, and then turned to May and Owen.

"He'll see you," she said. She gestured to an elevator on the right-hand side of the reception console. "That goes straight up to the penthouse suite."

May saw, to her surprise, that a black-uniformed security guard was standing outside the elevator. He checked them out with a suspicious glare as they approached.

"Police," May said, showing her badge again, and the man glanced over at the receptionist. Only when she nodded did he step reluctantly aside.

When they were in the elevator and riding up, Owen murmured, "It seems like that's his personal guard? Not the hotel's guard?"

"Yes, I got that impression too," May whispered back as the elevator whooshed upward.

When it stopped, the doors opened and a second black-uniformed security guard strode over to meet them. This, May assumed, was more of Bert Reed's personal security. He needed a lot of security!

What was so threatening to him? she wondered, as the guard led them down a short, wide corridor. When they reached the end, he knocked on a high, white-painted door.

"Come in," a male voice said.

The guard opened the door and May and Owen stepped into the reception room of the penthouse suite.

The walls were white. The floors were white marble. In the corner of the room was a leather lounge suite and coffee table, and in the center of the room was a circular white conference table. Chairs were arranged around it.

There were three people in the room.

Bert Reed, the hotel tycoon, was sitting at the head of the table. A strong-jawed man in his forties, he occupied the chair with the best view out of the windows onto the gardens and the golf course beyond. May's gaze was instantly drawn to his perfectly coiffed dark hair, which looked as sleek as if it had been oiled. He was casually dressed in a golf shirt and chinos.

Across from him was a strikingly beautiful woman in her thirties. She was wearing a black business suit with a crisp white shirt.

The third person was yet another security guard, standing to attention against the back wall.

The woman jumped up as they walked in.

"Good afternoon, Officers. Please have a seat. Mr. Reed, of Reed Leisure, welcomes you."

"Deputy May Moore," May said politely.

"Deputy Owen Lovell," Owen introduced himself.

"Afternoon," Reed said in a brusque, deep voice. "I don't have a lot of time. As I'm sure you're aware, this has been a very challenging day for us at Reed Leisure, and I'm in between meetings."

"I'm Taylor Ashby, Mr. Reed's personal assistant," the woman said. "Can I get you some tea?"

May was going to say no, but before she could, Owen said, "Yes, please."

Immediately May realized that was a good idea, as tea might enable them to stay longer. She had the impression that the clock was already ticking and that their police status meant nothing to Reed's schedule.

The assistant picked up a phone and spoke quickly into it.

"We're investigating a murder," May said. "I'm sure you have heard the very sad news that your architect was found dead this morning?"

Reed's face showed no reaction, but the beautiful assistant's slender body jerked visibly.

"It's tragic," Reed agreed. "I sincerely hope his killer can be found. Obviously, this has nothing to do with Reed Leisure, and must be a random crime. That's clearly why we need the hotel development to uplift the area. It's showing distinctive signs of urban blight. That crime is just one example."

He stared at them. May thought he looked smug. He certainly didn't look sad, or shocked, or show any normal reaction.

"Do you know of anyone who might have held a grudge against your architect? Someone who would want to kill him?" she asked.

Reed shook his head.

"No one comes to mind at all. He worked for us in a professional capacity. I have no idea what took place in his private life so perhaps you should focus your investigation on that side. I can't imagine who would want to do this."

A young platinum-haired woman in her early twenties, in a black and white uniform, appeared in the doorway with a tray. She carefully set the tray down on the table.

"Your tea, Mr. Reed," she said softly.

"Well, go ahead. Serve us," he ordered her impatiently.

The woman turned to May.

"Cream? Sugar?" she asked.

Her voice had a faint hint of Eastern Europe. May thought she looked intensely nervous. Her blue eyes looked scared. Her face was pale and tense.

To be fair, she thought she would also look nervous, having to pour tea for a short-tempered tycoon in this overdone setting.

"Cream and sugar, please," she said.

The maid poured tea for her, then for Owen, then for the assistant, and finally for Reed.

Then she stood up and left.

Glancing after her, May noted that the security guard standing by the wall took time off from his guarding duties to ogle her in a blatant and unpleasant way. Flushing, the maid looked away and hurried out of the room.

May seethed. She was so furious that she took a deep breath, intending to say something, but before she could get the words out, Reed continued smoothly.

"No doubt you are investigating at full speed in order to give us peace of mind on this matter. Have you come here to provide an update? Or do you need information?" He looked at the Rolex on his left wrist in a meaningful way.

It was time to get to the gist of their visit and May knew that even with the tea served, she'd better ask the questions she needed to, fast.

"We'd like to find out details on your insurance policy," May said.

"Our insurance policy?" Reed repeated, raising his eyebrows.

"Yes. I was told it pays out in the event that there's a catastrophe or unforeseen event that prevents construction from proceeding," May said. "I'd like to confirm if that is true. Will you be putting in a claim now that your architect is dead?"

There was a resounding silence in the room. The beautiful assistant looked shocked.

Reed's face darkened.

"If you believe I would do that, you are clearly not the caliber of investigators that will be able to solve the case," he said.

Owen drew in a sharp, angry breath. May did her best not to be offended by this derogatory statement, but rather to look past it and think about why Reed was saying this.

He was attacking. Did that mean he had something to hide?

"Take a good look at me," Reed said. "I don't need to kill someone to collect on an insurance policy. I am an extremely wealthy individual and a highly successful businessman. I don't need to murder anyone for money. I won't be claiming on the insurance as there's no need."

"Of course not," May said smoothly. "But there was that article that appeared recently which mentioned the hotel would never recoup its value."

Reed sneered.

"If that journalist has such a good understanding of business, why isn't she in business herself, instead of writing for a small-town gossip rag?"

"Umm," May said.

"I'm used to protests," he said. "I'm used to unfair criticism. I've heard it all before. I am building a hotel in a small town. Of course there will be a backlash from less successful people and those who can't adapt to progress. There's nothing unusual about that. But even so, I will sue that journalist as soon as I get around to it. For defamation."

"You think it's inaccurate?" May asked.

"Not just inaccurate. Totally defamatory. I am a respected businessman. I have a reputation to defend. The article paints me as some sort of incompetent with no knowledge of the market."

"So you think it's wrong?"

"Exactly," Reed said. "She's basing her article on a one-year projection. Within one year we won't yet break even. That's on a five-year plan. In five years we will be profitable. That's a long-term view of the business. We have a lot more in the pipeline. The second wing of the hotel includes the casino. Small-town folk will love that. It will bring excitement and glamour to their lives and give them hope for better prospects than the mundane, gray existence they lead, scraping out a living in their pointless little villages."

May heard Owen draw in a sharp breath at this scathing criticism. She had to admit, her hackles were rising too.

"Then we have the conferencing facilities set up so that big-city people can break away to experience the upmarket yet rural charms we will create for them. And then there are the other things we're working on to make sure the resort is top of mind."

He smiled. May didn't think it was a nice expression. She wasn't sure if the locals would like the other things, or even what they were. She remembered again what Owen had said about the strip clubs. That was the sort of smile it was. The smile of someone who was going to open a totally unsuitable venture in a location where it would be cheap to build, and by doing so, destroy the area.

"I see," she said, refusing to be sidetracked. "But about this policy. Could you explain it to me?"

Now Reed looked seriously angry.

"I do not need to explain my insurance affairs to you! I have others working on the hotel's design. Danny Charter is not irreplaceable."

"I need more clarity on the hotel and the financial situation." May stood firm as Reed raged.

"I am going to sue you! Do you think you can't be sued because you're the cops? I can and will. Do you know who Devonshire, Clark and Bissett are?"

"Yes, I do know them," May began, but he wasn't listening to her.

"They're the biggest law firm in Minnesota and I have them on retainer for all my local issues," he raged. He glanced around at the guard by the wall. The guard moved a step closer. "Leave! Now!"

The environment was beginning to feel decidedly threatening, May realized. She wasn't going to leave, though. This was even more reason to stay.

But at that moment, Owen's phone buzzed.

He glanced at it and then said, "I'd better take this."

"Take it outside! I've had enough of the both of you!"

May stood up.

She wanted to protest and stand her ground, but she was now worried that this call was serious news. There was something in Owen's face that told her it might be important.

"We'll step outside. But don't think for a moment that we won't come back if we need to," May warned.

"You won't get in here again. Police or not!" Reed taunted.

May and Owen hustled out, and as soon as the penthouse door had slammed behind them, Owen took the call.

May saw his face go pale as he spoke briefly. Then he turned to May.

"There's been another body found," he whispered. "Killed in a very similar way. This time it's a woman who was staying at a luxury lodge near Misty Hills. They've just called it in. We need to head there immediately."

CHAPTER TEN

Owen thought it was weird, in this case, how they seemed to be shuttling between a bunch of luxury establishments. What was going on? Why were these wealthy people being targeted? Never had he thought that this peaceful community would ever experience such a level of violent crime. Any murder was terrible. But a killer targeting the wealthy, he knew from experience, would bring a whole new level of panic and blame. This serial killing spree would make news headlines, in all the wrong ways.

What had triggered it? he wondered, confused, as they pulled up outside the magnificent entrance of Rushway River Lodge, slotting in between an ambulance and a coroner's van who he guessed had probably just arrived.

He felt they didn't know enough yet, and that they were stumbling around in the dark, but he was sure that May would get to the gist of it.

She was as sharp as a tack. She was pretty. She was super-capable. And above all, she was kind. Owen had seen how she cared for the people who were in need, the ones who couldn't help themselves, those who needed a hand.

That had already earned her all his admiration. He was proud to have her as his investigation partner. It was because of people like May that he'd chosen to quit the field of accounting and move into law enforcement, where there was more chance of helping people and making a difference. So he thought, anyway.

They hurried inside.

The receptionist immediately rushed over. She was young and well-groomed and looked devastated.

"Are you the police? This is so terrible. Let me take you to the room where it happened."

"Is the victim a guest here?" Owen asked.

"Yes, she is. A guest who arrived yesterday evening. I have all her details here," the receptionist said, passing over a sheet of paper. "It's this way, she's in the Waterlily Suite. I am so upset. I just can't believe it's happened to one of our guests. It seems like someone broke in and attacked her. And then left her in the tub with the water running. That's how housekeeping was alerted. They saw the water overflowing and went in to see."

Owen paced down the corridor behind her, feeling unsettled by her words. This was extremely disturbing. Was it another serial case? he wondered. If so, why was this killer targeting wealthy people in upmarket hotel locations?

He glanced back at May. She was as cool as a cucumber, but she was clearly studying the scene ahead.

As they approached the luxury room, Owen saw it was already a hive of activity.

It was large and magnificently appointed. A four-poster bed was the centerpiece of the room. It had huge windows overlooking the forested grounds of the estate. And on the far side of the room, an arched doorway led into a bathroom.

There, Owen saw Andy Baker on site, leaning over the bathtub. Sheriff Jack was standing nearby, watching solemnly and making notes.

They stopped inside the door and put on head covers, foot covers, and gloves.

"It looks as if the killer gained access through the sliding door that was open," a cop from the Misty Hills department told them. "Maybe the victim left it open. It doesn't show any sign of being forced."

Owen watched as May moved forward into the large luxurious bathroom.

It was decorated in a stunning contemporary style, with black and white check tiles on the floor and wall, and chrome fittings. There was a large, free-standing bath tub with a shower to the side of it. The floor was still slippery with water.

Owen wasn't sure he was ready to see this. He had only seen a few other murder scenes in his life. Would he ever get used to it?

May was so matter of fact, so focused on her job, she didn't seem to be fazed. He drew his strength from her.

He moved forward. Sheriff Jack gave him and May a nod of welcome, his face stern. Then Owen took a look.

The woman was fully clothed in a gorgeous burgundy dress. She was wearing expensive jewelry and earrings. And she seemed to have an injury on the back of her head that reminded him a lot of the one on the body he'd pulled out of the lake yesterday.

Both victims had been hit from behind and then drowned. One in a lake, one in a bathtub.

He watched, feeling a sense of apprehension, as Andy Baker opened the woman's mouth.

"Now this is interesting," Andy Baker murmured. "We have a serial, for sure."

Owen felt his heart accelerate as Andy pulled out another folded five-dollar bill.

He handed it to May, who took it and opened it up, holding it carefully in her gloved hands as she frowned down at it.

Owen had a sense of foreboding as he watched her expression. He could tell she was thinking hard, and that she was puzzled.

"What do you think this means?" Owen asked.

"I'm not sure," May admitted. "It definitely means something, though. The money is a message. It has significance to the killer."

What significance? Owen wondered. Finding out would be crucial. It would enable them to solve this crime. Leaving a message meant the kills were being made for a reason. But what reason?

May walked back to the suite's main door where the receptionist was waiting, looking nervous. Owen followed her, glad to get out of the bathroom.

"Have you or the house guests seen anyone suspicious around here? Anyone sneaking around in the lodge, or on the grounds?" May asked the receptionist. "Any guests who checked out suddenly?"

"No. We confirmed this with security as soon as the body was found. We had a look at the camera footage from the gate, and our security guards are patrolling the perimeter in golf carts as we speak. No one else has seen anything so far."

"We will need to get all the footage from the security cameras," May said.

"That's no problem. But I hope it gets you results. You see, we do think that someone could have gotten into the estate on foot and left again, undetected. We have walkways and paths, horse riding trails, and mountain biking trails that leave the estate and traverse the wider area."

Owen nodded. With grounds so large and an on-site golf course, there were going to be numerous opportunities for a killer to simply walk off site and head back to a vehicle parked elsewhere.

"What's the victim's name?" May asked Owen quietly. "They gave us her check-in details a few minutes ago, so let's have a look. Even though it's miles away from the Lakeside Heights hotel, perhaps there's a connection somewhere."

Owen thought that was a good question. They had been so focused on examining the scene, and then picking up the shocking similarities between the crimes, they hadn't yet had time to look at the identity of the victim. But that was important. Perhaps there was a link that would take them further.

Owen opened the piece of paper they had been given.

"It says here the victim is—" He paused, shocked. Then he read the page again just in case he'd gotten it wrong.

"May, look here!" he said.

She moved closer, staring down at the page.

"This might be a coincidence. But it says here that this guest's name is Madeline Reed."

May was clearly as puzzled by the name as Owen was.

"Reed?" she said to Owen in a soft, incredulous voice.

"It can't be!" he whispered back. "Surely just a coincidence?"

Owen was totally confused. Was there a link between this woman and the obnoxious tycoon who'd recently hustled them out of his penthouse? If so, why was she staying here, in a hotel that wasn't owned by Reed Leisure?

"We need to find out urgently whether there is a connection," May said. "If there proves to be one, it puts these crimes into a whole new light."

CHAPTER ELEVEN

"Look here," May said to Owen excitedly. They were sitting side by side in the car, in the parking lot outside Rushway River Lodge, using her laptop to log into the police information databases.

She couldn't believe what the search had just uncovered.

Madeline Reed was Bert Reed's younger sister.

"His sister!" Owen said incredulously.

Immediately, May messaged Sheriff Jack to tell him about this bombshell.

As she keyed in the words, May felt a sense of unreality. Someone was targeting Reed Leisure. There was absolutely no doubt about it. And they'd gone to the lengths of following Madeline Reed all the way here to where she was staying. This wasn't just a crime inflicted on random people at the hotel, but rather people involved with the hotel business.

"Reed couldn't have done it himself. He wouldn't have been able to in terms of timing," May said. "He was at the Mount Amethyst hotel in meetings."

"Could he have arranged both their deaths?" Owen asked. "A rich guy like that could have hired an assassin."

"Yes, we can't rule that out. But he'd need a motive, and apart from the insurance policy there isn't a clear motive. At any rate, not yet. So if the sister was somehow covered by that policy, then yes. But otherwise, no."

"My gut feel is no," Owen agreed.

"I say the same. I don't think Bert Reed knew about this when we met him," May said. "I think if we focus too hard on him, we might overlook important motives that other people have."

"Agreed," Owen said.

"I wonder how he'll feel when he hears," May said.

"Surely he'll be devastated if he finds out his sister has been killed? He'll want to help us if he can. After all, she was his sister," Owen said.

"I wonder what their relationship is like, though. Why was she in a totally different lodge? Are they friendly? Are they estranged? Why not stay at the same place as him? Or at his hotel?" May wondered. "He might have an alibi for the crime but it doesn't necessarily mean they were close."

"There is something going on here. There has to be a reason she was targeted. What is this family hiding?" Owen asked.

May looked up as Sheriff Jack walked out and headed for their car. He was shaking his head, looking as perturbed as May felt.

"This has to be related to the hotel chain somehow, May. Do you think Bert Reed knew his sister was likely to be targeted? As he's the closest next of kin, one of us has to go and tell him the news. If he doesn't know it already, of course, because who knows what motives are at play here?"

"We were thinking the same," May agreed.

"I'm wondering what the best way of telling Reed will be."

May considered the possibilities.

"He's just seen me and Owen. It didn't go well, and I don't think we'll be the best choice to go back again."

Sheriff Jack nodded.

"I will go and break the news to him, and take one of our other officers with me. And I'll observe his reaction carefully."

"Thank you," May said. "I hope you'll pick something up from him."

Sheriff Jack turned and headed for his own car.

"Where are we going to go in the meantime?" Owen asked.

"I have an idea," May said. "I want to go and speak to those lawyers that Bert Reed threatened us with. Perhaps they can tell us more about what the family's been involved with."

*

It was four-thirty p.m. when May and Owen pulled up outside the head office of Devonshire, Clark and Bissett. The head office was located in Meadowtown in Tamarack County, a place May knew fairly well.

She walked in, and was glad to see the person she remembered was still at the reception desk. Small-town life strikes again, she thought. This connection could possibly prove useful. It was, in fact, one of the reasons she'd decided to come here.

"Hello, Christa," she greeted the brown-haired, blue-eyed woman who'd been in her class for most of school.

"May Moore! Good to see you!" Christa smiled. "I heard you were promoted recently?"

53

May nodded, thinking that sometimes, in a small-town setting, it was nice the way word got around.

"That's right. I'm county deputy now."

"That's seriously great. I'm super-impressed. And are you here on business today?"

"Yes, I am."

"Who are you here to see?"

"Whichever of your bosses deals with Reed Leisure and the Reed family."

Christa's eyes widened and May saw she knew about some of what was going on.

"That would be Mr. Devonshire."

"Is he available for a quick chat with the police?"

"Let me check."

Christa got up and rushed down the corridor.

A moment later, May heard the click of her heels as she rushed back again.

"Mr. Devonshire can have a brief meeting with you in the first boardroom to your right." She indicated the passage she'd just returned from.

"Thank you," May said.

She and Owen hurried down the hall and went into the boardroom. There, six leather seats surrounded a polished oak table. May and Owen took seats facing the door.

"I hope this works out," May whispered to Owen.

"I hope so too," he whispered back.

"If you think of a question, ask it," May advised. "We both need to do the talking here."

"Right," Owen said, nodding.

Footsteps sounded outside and the door opened. Mr. Devonshire walked in. He was a tall man with silver hair and a neatly trimmed gray beard. He was dressed in a black suit, a gray tie, and a white shirt.

"Good afternoon, Officers. I understand you're here on official police business? What can I do for you?"

He pulled up another chair and sat down, facing them across the table.

"I understand that your firm represents the Reed family business," May continued.

"That's right. We're on retainer to deal with all their legal matters," he explained.

"I don't know if you are yet aware that Madeline Reed has recently been murdered?" May said.

"What?" Mr. Devonshire nearly jumped out of his chair. He clearly had not known, and was deeply shocked. "Madeline? Murdered? When? I knew about Danny, but her?"

"Just a couple of hours ago. She was murdered in the same way as he was. Hit on the head and then drowned. She was staying at Rushway River Lodge, and they found her body in the bathtub."

"This is appalling," Mr. Devonshire muttered. He'd turned pale.

"There must be some reason why they were both killed in such a specific way," May explained.

"Absolutely," Mr. Devonshire said, nodding vigorously.

"We need to find out what the common thread is. I understand that certain information may be privileged, but I'm hoping that given the seriousness of the situation, you'll be able to tell us some of the facts," May appealed.

Mr. Devonshire rubbed his chin thoughtfully. "What facts?" he asked.

"It seems very likely that these crimes are related to the Reed Leisure business, or to the Reed family," May said. "Danny was killed on the shores of the lake near the new hotel, but the killer targeted Madeline Reed while she was staying elsewhere, and that means that Madeline must have been known to the killer."

"That's likely, yes. However, I'm not sure what I can tell you. The matters we handled for the Reeds were all routine. Very routine. Legal matters such as contracts, a couple of warnings for defamation, and one or two in-house matters. We dealt with their staffing disputes and the like."

May persevered anyway. "What were the recent disputes? Anything involving Danny or Madeline?"

"Not that I recall," Mr. Devonshire said, but he suddenly sat very still and May felt sure he was lying.

"Have you been involved with the family's other business interests?" Owen asked. "Anything untoward there? Any recent conflicts, disagreements, bad blood? Anyone forced into a sale or a position they were unhappy with?"

May could see in his face that there were answers. But he wasn't giving them. Instead, he shut down.

"Nothing that rings alarm bells for me," he insisted. "We deal only with issues here in Minnesota. They have other law firms on contract for their New York affairs."

"What was Madeline's role in the business? Did she have a role?"

"No official role. I know she accompanied her brother to some of the launches and openings," Devonshire said smoothly.

"What was their relationship like?"

He shook his head. "I have no idea about that. I really can't say."

Owen looked disappointed. May, however, was ready to move onto her plan B. She'd guessed they might get nothing from the lawyer, but it had still been worth asking.

In fact, now it was even more important to keep digging, because the fact the lawyer wasn't talking meant there were things he didn't want them to know about.

She checked her watch. Listening, she heard footsteps and the jingle of keys from beyond the door.

May got up quickly.

"Thank you so much for your time," she told the attorney. "I appreciate your help."

He nodded gravely.

"Sorry I couldn't have been of more help to you in such a tragic situation. I'm going to call Mr. Reed immediately and give him our condolences."

He watched as the two of them left. May closed the door behind him.

"Well, that was a real pity," Owen muttered as they headed past the now empty reception desk. "I'm sure he knew more, but there was no way he was going to tell. Now we'll never find out."

May shook her head.

"There's another way we can find out, if we're quick. Follow me."

Instead of walking out of the grand front entrance, she took the stairs that led down to the basement parking lot.

There, if she hurried, she hoped she would find the source she needed.

CHAPTER TWELVE

The basement parking lot was a very different place from the showy frontage of the law firm. Down here, it was dark and damp and nearly deserted. Only a few cars were parked in the shadowy space.

May saw a BMW, a Mercedes, and a Porsche. The cheapest of the four, an Alfa Romeo, was getting ready to leave. The engine started and headlamps flashed.

May broke into a run. She jumped in front of the car and held up her hand. Owen pounded up beside her as brakes squealed. The window buzzed down and Christa looked curiously out.

"What's up?" she said.

"I need your help," May said breathlessly.

"My help? Sure." Christa frowned at her, puzzled.

May decided there was only going to be one way to do this. She turned to Owen.

"Will you take my car back to the police department?" She handed him the keys.

"Sure," Owen said after a pause.

May climbed in the passenger side of the Alfa Romeo, next to Christa.

"Will you give me a ride to the police department?" she asked her old school friend.

Christa looked more confused than ever. "Sure. I mean, but why?"

May fastened her seatbelt and spoke in a low voice.

"We really need this case solved, Christa. There is a murderer at work. We don't know who's going to die next. It could be anyone linked to the Reeds. It could even be someone from this law firm. Until we know more, everyone's at risk, and I mean everyone."

Her eyes widened. "Of course."

"Your boss couldn't tell us some of the facts, because he's bound by confidentiality agreements. But I know you probably know as much, or more, about the clients as he does. Receptionists always do."

Christa drove out of the garage, glancing at May suspiciously.

"Like what? I can't give you any documents, any facts and figures."

May shook her head. "I don't need that. I need your impression about things. And background information. That would be so helpful," she appealed.

"I don't know if I should," Christa argued. "If my boss didn't say anything, and I talk, then I'm going to be in trouble."

"I won't say it came from you. I promise that."

"It still feels wrong," she protested.

May thought back.

"Remember that time Penny tried to bully you in school, and you smacked her upside the head, and she tried to get you expelled?"

Christa nodded. "I remember that."

"Remember I was the one who stood up for you and explained you'd been bullied, even though it got me in trouble too?"

"Yes, I remember," Christa said.

"No one believed your side of the story until I spoke up."

"Okay," Christa said doubtfully.

"That's why I'm asking you to help us. Someone needs to speak up. More people are bound to get killed if we don't crack this case."

Christa was silent for a long moment, driving carefully.

May upped the pressure. "You're a strong person. You fight for people who can't stand up for themselves. I remember how you were back then. You would never let anyone push you around. You'd fight back. And that's exactly how you are now. You fight for the people who need it," May said. "If telling us something you know can help catch a murderer, that's the sort of thing you would do. Right?"

"I guess so," Christa said doubtfully.

"The truth's important. Withholding information that could help us is what's wrong. I'm just asking you to do the right thing now. If you do the right thing, you might well end up basically solving this case."

She could see that appealed to Christa.

"Okay. I can try. I really don't know much, though. They keep all the dealings with that firm very confidential, and to be honest, it's bothered me before now. Why does everything need to be kept so tightly under wraps? I've wondered myself what really goes on."

"The relationship between Mr. Reed and his sister. What was it like? What was your impression?" May asked.

Christa frowned. "Not close. They didn't seem to like each other very much, but for some reason my impression is that they did do a fair amount of business together. I think they had to start running some affairs through the company, and through other people, for some reason. They seemed to change that recently. Madeline wanted to take a step back."

"Which other people?"

"I don't know. It was a snippet of conversation I overheard, and I think it was someone else within the company that was going to take over some of what she did. Whatever that was."

She pulled onto the main road. Now they were following Owen back to the police department.

"Did Madeline have any role within the company?" May asked curiously. What exactly was being taken over? she wondered.

Again, Christa made a face.

"No official role, but it was strange how involved she seemed to be. Whenever there was a function or an event she'd get dressed up and head off. I first thought she was just a leech who enjoyed partying on Reed Leisure's dime. But I then decided Mr. Reed didn't seem like the kind of person to give anyone a free lunch, not even his sister, so I decided there must be some kind of trade-off."

"What else?" May said, feeling encouraged.

"She made a lot of travel arrangements which Reed Leisure paid for. She was forever going off to exotic places like Belarus, Latvia, Lithuania."

"Is that so?" May asked. "For work? Or for vacation?"

"I think they were charged as recruitment trips, but I have no idea why."

May filed that information away. Something about it was niggling at her mind.

"Anything else?" she asked. "Anything about Danny? He was also killed. Can you think of anyone who'd have a motive?"

Christa thought about that for a few moments.

"He did have a fight recently. Someone from the hotel called us because Danny ended up shouting and swearing that he was going to take them down. We are always called to mediate in those situations"

"Who was it?"

At last, May thought, they seemed to be getting somewhere.

"It was the personnel manager. Lewis Brooks. They had a fight over a woman. I think she worked for the hotel, and she was Lewis's girlfriend, and Danny made a pass at her. But I might be wrong about that. It was definitely something to do with a woman who worked there, though. They came in here for mediation and both of them were yelling at each other so I overheard some of what they said. But I don't know more than that. My private opinion, just between you and me, is that Danny is quite a womanizer. He's flirted with me in a nasty, entitled way when he's been in here. You shouldn't speak badly of the dead, but I didn't like how he made me feel."

"I would also have felt uneasy," May sympathized. "The fight between them. How serious was it?"

"Look, to me it was just one of those things. We handle conflict issues fairly often. It wasn't as serious as some have been."

But Danny had ended up being murdered in a strange way, May thought. Something, or someone, had certainly thought that what he'd done had been serious enough.

They had now reached the police department and she couldn't think of any more questions. She didn't think Christa had more information to give, but was grateful for what she'd obtained.

"Thanks a lot. You've been so helpful. And I'll make sure it stays under wraps," she said.

She climbed out and closed the door.

Owen was climbing out of her car, so she walked over to him. The sun was setting and a fresh breeze was cooling down the warm summer air. What passed for rush hour in this small town had already come and gone, and the streets were quiet.

"Did you get anything from the receptionist?" he asked.

"Yes. But I don't know how helpful it's going to be," May admitted. "I found out that the sister is a bit of a freeloader, but she does do some work for the hotel."

"She does?" Owen asked.

"Yes. I don't know what work it is, but I am wondering if she maybe sources cheap labor for the hotel. As she seems to travel on 'recruitment trips' to Eastern Europe frequently."

"Is it legal to do that?"

May shrugged. "It would depend if it's done correctly. For all I know they are using a loophole to save on costs somewhere down the line. That might be worth investigating, though. I mean, two people have been killed in a very strange way. So there has to be something underhanded or wrong going on. There really does."

Again, something niggled at her mind. She wished she could pin down what was bothering her.

"What are we missing, May?" Owen asked.

"I can't stop thinking that there must be something I've seen or heard recently that's relevant to this. I hope my brain puts two and two together."

"Maybe we should run all of those people through the system?" Owen asked. "Madeline Reed, Danny Charter, and Lewis Brooks? Perhaps one of them has some sort of record. That could take us further."

"Good idea," May said.

They headed inside, and Owen hurried through to the back office. There, he sat down and logged onto the computer system.

"Madeline Reed, Madeline Reed. Let's do her first."

May peered over his shoulder as he searched. But it seemed the system was coming up blank.

"She's done nothing," he said. "I'm going to look for the others."

He tapped more keys. "Nope. Danny Charter has no recorded offenses. And nor does the only Lewis Brooks who resides in Minnesota."

But May's mind was on that international travel.

"Madeline Reed traveled a lot. And you know what I'm remembering? Christa said that they started running some of her transactions through the business, and through other people. She didn't say who or why. But perhaps it was because they had to. Because Madeline was being scrutinized in some way."

"There might be more to discover," Owen agreed. "But how can you find out what it is?"

With a thud of her heart, May realized what she needed. Unfortunately, the international travel angle pointed straight to one organization, and one particular person, that she would need to ask for help.

The problem was that she really, really didn't want to.

Was she going to be able to make this call?

CHAPTER THIRTEEN

Feeling extremely reluctant, May dialed Kerry's number. She didn't want her sister involved in this case at all. She didn't want her to interfere or try to take over, or derail the investigation.

But she needed information that only the FBI databases could provide.

Listening to the phone ring, May wondered how best to approach this delicate situation.

Kerry answered sounding upbeat.

"Hello, sis! I've just been in town, catching up with a couple of old friends. I need a favor from you!"

From her? May thought it was going to be the other way around.

"What favor?" she asked cautiously.

"Look, I'm in town at the moment. In fact, I'm walking down Main Street. How about I meet you at Dan's Bar in five?"

"Sure. I can be there in two," May said, glancing down the road. She hadn't been in Dan's Bar for a while. And handsome Dan, the owner, had been her unrequited crush for years. Thoughts of him surged. Hopes flamed. Perhaps this would be a good opportunity to see him again, and she could move the situation forward.

"I'm going to talk to Kerry," she told Owen. "She might be able to give us the information we need. I shouldn't be long. Half an hour, maybe? Then I'll come back here and let you know what I found."

"Okay," he said. "I'll wait here for Sheriff Jack to get back. Perhaps Mr. Reed gave him more information when he told him about his sister's death."

"We'll catch up later," May agreed. She turned and headed out of the police department, walking quickly down the street toward the bar.

At this hour, there was already a buzz at Dan's Bar, and she heard the music and voices before she reached the well decked out corner building. She stepped into the glamorous interior, immediately feeling her heart speed up as Dan gave her his trademark flashing smile. With his strong-jawed face, his crisp, perfectly cut hair, and his muscular arms, he always looked the part of the dashing barman.

"How's my favorite policewoman?" he asked.

Was she really his favorite? May wondered, with a nervous twist of her insides. At that point, light suddenly dawned. She was the only policewoman in this town!

"Hi, Dan. I'm great. It's good to see you again." She smiled, feeling herself start to blush.

"It's been a long time. I've missed seeing you here. How have you been?"

"I'm doing great," she said. "You?"

Her cheeks were burning now. She'd felt so capable when talking to Christa. So ready to say what needed to be said. And now, in front of her good-looking crush, she was totally tongue-tied. Why couldn't she come across as clever, witty, funny, or better still, flirtatious?

"Never better. What can I get you?"

"A coffee, please," May said, aware she might still have a few hours of work ahead.

"How's your sister?" he asked as he moved to the coffee machine. "I heard she's in town?"

May felt her heart sink.

She had to face the harsh reality that she was involved in a crush triangle!

She was crushing on Dan, Dan was crushing on Kerry, and Kerry couldn't care less about either of them, because she had a new handsome, wealthy fiancé.

"Kerry's in town. She came to tell my folks she got engaged," she said to Dan.

She saw the disappointment etch itself into his face.

"Engaged?" he said.

For a moment, May wondered if perhaps now that he knew this about Kerry, he'd pay her more attention. Perhaps now she'd get somewhere with him.

But then she realized how that made her feel. It made her feel small and inadequate, as if she was only ever expecting second best, and somebody else's cast-offs.

May felt something inside herself, something she hadn't even known was there, start to strengthen.

Did she really want to be trapped in an unspoken crush with a guy who was clearly infatuated with her sister, and wasn't ever more than polite and friendly to her?

That was a hard thought to have to accept. She wasn't sure if she was ready for it.

"Yes. Engaged," May said firmly. "She's very happy about it."

At that moment, Kerry breezed in.

"Hi, sis! Sorry, I don't have long. I have to get back to the folks' place by six to take a conference call. Work never waits. There are still cases to be followed up on. Still important developments I need to keep track of."

She ran a hand through her blond hair. The diamond flashed.

May saw Dan's gaze on her, at once infatuated and devastated.

"I'd love a beer, please, Dan," she said.

"Coming right up." May thought Dan mentally shook himself as he turned away.

"Anyway, the favor I need from you," Kerry said.

"What is it?" May asked, hoping she might have some room to bargain.

"Brandon's finally managed to get away from work. He's flying here first thing tomorrow morning. And I still don't have a car! The day ran away with me. Could you take me to the airport tomorrow so we can meet him?"

May stared at her in consternation.

"I'm sorry. I can't," she said. "I'm busy with a case. I'm going to be working on it from early tomorrow."

"Oh." Kerry didn't look that upset. "In that case, could you loan me your car? It would be nice to arrive there with a decent set of wheels. Mum and Dad's car is really elderly and I like driving fast, as you know. It's on my to-do list to buy them a new car. I just haven't actioned it yet," she said firmly.

May wanted so badly to say no to her sister again. She'd had the whole day to make a plan to get a car. May was busy, she was working, she was on the trail of a murderer. She needed her wheels and she didn't like the thought of Kerry speeding off in her treasured car.

But she couldn't refuse. Not when she had a trade-off to make. She'd have to loan her prized wheels to her sister, even though it burned her to do so.

Dan placed Kerry's beer and her coffee on the bar counter.

May stirred in cream and sugar.

"I guess you can borrow it," she said reluctantly. "But please, drive it carefully."

"Don't worry." Kerry beamed. "I'll return it in top condition."

May wasn't so sure she'd get it back at all, given Kerry's driving skills.

"I'd appreciate that. And no speeding fines, please. It's embarrassing, not to mention illegal, when people see the deputy's car speeding," May said firmly.

"Oh, yes. I never thought about that. But anyway, you want to tell me anything about the case?" Kerry then asked, as Dan turned away to serve a new customer. "Perhaps there's something I can help you with?"

Kerry sipped her beer. May knew what she was thinking. Kerry was always the one who called the shots. Always the one who kicked in and ran things, and the one who made decisions. She didn't want to tell her anything else because she was sure that as soon as she did, Kerry would be desperate to muscle in.

"It's a murder case," she admitted.

"A murder?" Kerry said, her eyes widening. "Oh, how unusual for this town. You're handling a real case at last! I'm sure it'll be a great learning experience for you. You'll learn a lot about running an investigation from the ground up. I can advise you, of course. Perhaps we can go through it quickly. Do you have any leads?"

This was May's chance.

"I have a lead," she said.

Kerry leaned forward, interested.

"What is it?"

But May shook her head. She couldn't tell Kerry. However, she had to ask her for the favor.

"I don't want to say more. Not in here," she said, looking around as if one of the nearby locals might overhear if she did. "But I need some background, and I was wondering if you could help provide it."

Kerry looked surprised, as if she hadn't expected May to come back at her like that.

"What background?" she asked.

"On one of the murder victims."

"There's more than one?" Kerry seemed even more intrigued. "Is this a serial? If so, shouldn't we be involved? That's the FBI's domain."

"The victims are linked, and they are both involved with the same company, so it points to a motive related to the workplace, rather than a true serial crime," May said.

Kerry nodded, looking disappointed.

"But the victim I'm looking for some background on is a woman who made frequent trips out of the country and I am wondering if she was possibly a person of interest to the FBI. If you tracked her, or her transactions."

"Well, you'll need to tell me the full circumstances," Kerry said bossily. "I can see I'll have to get involved. This is definitely not looking like a local issue any longer."

"No," May said firmly. "Right now, I just need to know the background. As a favor. Like loaning you the car."

For a moment, Kerry looked absolutely furious. As if May had outmaneuvered her.

May knew they were all the way back in their sister rival territory. This was a place they seemed to have been their whole life, prompted mainly by their mother's habit of pitting the daughters against each other in a competitive way, to ensure each one tried their hardest.

May didn't want her sister to be mad. And she desperately needed her to agree to this. She didn't want to have to explain anything more, or for Kerry to muscle in on the case.

So she guessed it would come down to how badly Kerry needed that car, and whether she was prepared to put her own ego aside to help.

May sipped her coffee and waited, looking as calm and unbothered as she could. Inside she was shaking. This mattered so much to her.

Kerry didn't speak. Her face was mutinous.

"Kerry," May said quietly. "This is really important to me. I need to do this. I want to do it with my team and not get the FBI involved in managing it. If there's a need for the FBI to be involved, I will call you first, I promise. But at the moment we're just getting information, and I don't want to lose this lead. It's my first chance on a big case. And I've never had a chance to work on a murder case that I'm officially managing, as the county's deputy," she added truthfully. The previous murder case, her boss had handed over to the FBI.

Finally, Kerry nodded.

"Alright. I'll help. What do you need to know?"

May felt a surge of relief.

With her sister's help, she hoped they would uncover information they needed to get further in this troubling case.

CHAPTER FOURTEEN

May walked back to the police precinct feeling hopeful. Kerry was going to make the call somewhere quiet, and then she was going to walk down the road and take May's truck back to their parents' place. It would be hers tonight and tomorrow morning.

May hoped she'd get it back in one piece.

She headed into the police department, where Owen was finishing off on a call.

"I've just spoken to Sheriff Jack," he told May. "Reed was very shocked to hear his sister was killed. Jack said his shock seemed genuine, but that he wasn't as torn up about it as he expected he would be. So I don't think they were close, and Jack also suspects he knows more than he's telling. But he couldn't get any more information out of him."

That seemed typical behavior for Bert Reed, who seemed to keep his secrets close. But May hoped their ace up the sleeve, aka her sister, might breach his defenses.

"Kerry is going to ask one of her colleagues to search the FBI databases," May said. "She's going to see if Madeline's name appears there at all, if she was a person of interest. She'll call if there's any information." May sighed. "But in return, she wants to borrow my car. She needs it tomorrow early morning. So I've given her the keys and she'll take it back to my parents' house. Could you give me a ride home later?"

"Sure!" Owen said eagerly. "I'll gladly do that. Will you need a ride to work tomorrow, too?"

"I'm hoping I might have it back by then. But if not I'll call you. Thanks so much."

She smiled at him, feeling glad that he was on her side.

At that moment, her phone rang. It was Kerry. With her heart leaping, May grabbed up the call.

"Well, sis, I have some interesting information," Kerry said.

"What is it?" May switched the phone to speaker as Owen hustled over, pulling up a chair and reaching for a pen.

"Madeline Reed is a person of interest to the FBI, due to her frequent trips out of the country and also the movement of large sums of money in and out of her accounts. There were a couple of minor reports made a while ago that alerted us to her. Unfortunately I can't get into those at short notice so I don't know what the actual transactions are. But she is on our radar. And we've been monitoring her bank accounts. Recently, however, there has been less activity there, apart from one large payment she made, which is rather interesting."

"Who was that made to?"

"Well, this is where it gets complicated," Kerry said. "Because I can't tell you confidential information. Not if I'm not involved in the case."

May waited, her heart thudding. Was her sister going to insist on getting involved?

"I can just say that you need to look into a local person's bank accounts more closely. As if you do, you might find a large payment went through there," Kerry said cagily.

"And who exactly is that person?" May asked.

"Well, it's a local journalist," Kerry said.

"And?"

May waited expectantly.

"That's all I can say," Kerry concluded triumphantly. "I'm sure if you guys spend a few days on the case, researching your people, you will come up with it in due course. It might take a while. Of course, you could always ask the FBI to come on board and handle your case. Then I'd tell you."

There was a resounding silence.

"Kerry," May said, swallowing. "You promised."

"I did," Kerry agreed, her voice innocent. "But you have the choice, sis."

"You promised. You said you'd give me the information," May said in a small voice.

"And I have," Kerry said. "I gave it to you. You just didn't accept the whole package, which includes me. Next time, don't make assumptions."

"Kerry, you said you'd help," May said, her voice shaking a little.

"And I did, sister dear," Kerry said, her voice full of mock sorrow. "I told you all I know. And now I'd like to get in your car and go home. Tell me if you find anything out."

May stared at Owen, seeing her own helplessness reflected in his gaze.

She felt devastated. She'd had so much hope for tomorrow, believing she could at least make some inquiries about the money, but Kerry had taken yet another example of big sister power over her.

May felt a wave of anger rise up and surge through her. Kerry had them over a barrel.

She was having fun stringing her along. She was annoyed that she hadn't been brought into the loop on the case and was determined to take a piece of it.

And it was because of that that she was withholding information.

"Well, I can't let you into the case," May said at last. "There's no reason to do that. We have to manage it ourselves up until there is a real reason for FBI involvement, if that happens at all. But I'm surprised by you. I thought you might have some information that could help catch a killer."

"That's all I can say," Kerry reiterated. "I'm sure you'll be able to figure it out, with a little effort. It was a very large payment. Might even have been around the five-hundred-thousand-dollar mark."

May's heart sped up.

"You think it was bribe money?" she asked.

Kerry sighed. "In my experience, and given that it was paid to a journalist, it's far more likely to be blackmail."

May frowned. "Blackmail for what?"

"I don't know," Kerry said.

May waited, but there was no more information forthcoming.

"Well, the FBI can't be involved in the case," May said.

Kerry laughed. "That's so silly, May. You're being an idiot, and very shortsighted, not to let me get involved. Anyway, I've given you the hint you needed. Now you can take it further, or not."

May stared at the phone in dismay. She could imagine her sister's grin widening at her silence.

Anger and frustration coursed through her. She'd been used.

Her sister had made a big deal of giving them information and then withheld it, knowing that they had no choice but to let her have her way.

Worst of all, she had the car keys already, so May couldn't renege on the deal about the pickup. Not that she would want to do such a thing. She just wanted Kerry to keep her side of the bargain!

Feeling helpless and unsure what to do, she slumped forward, putting her head in her hands. She tried to concentrate on the information she had. The FBI had been monitoring Madeline's bank accounts. They were tracking big payments out of her account, and frequent international travel. No doubt there were other reasons but Kerry wasn't saying those. May guessed that if Reed Leisure was also involved in strip clubs, there might be some money laundering going on, but that was just a guess.

And recently a huge payment, most likely blackmail, had been made to a local journo.

Finally, May's mind started to turn. There was only one journalist she knew of who had intimate knowledge of the Reeds' affairs and who had published articles on it.

That journalist was Emily Oxman.

"Is it Emily?" May asked innocently.

The outraged gasp and shocked silence she received in response told her she'd hit a bull's-eye.

"Thanks, sis. We'll get going on that then," May said. "Appreciate the information. So kind of you. Enjoy the pickup."

She ended the call, feeling a rush of relief. Finally they'd come to a breakthrough. They were on the right track.

Owen stood up with a big grin on his face.

"May, that was brilliant. Brilliant! So Emily Oxman was blackmailing Madeline? How are we going to research this further, and find out why?"

"We're going to need to go and confront her about this. Let's look up her address, and while we're at it, see if there are any other details on her that might be important," May said.

CHAPTER FIFTEEN

Huddled over her laptop, side by side with Owen on his, May searched back through Emily's profile and history. She wanted to find out her address, but she was also interested in any other information that might be available.

Because there was surely a chance that Emily might be the killer. If so, what had motivated her to commit these crimes? Was there any association between her and the Reeds, apart from a simple role as a journalist?

"According to this site, she's thirty-four," Owen said. "She seems to have been working as a journalist for more than a decade. She's divorced after being married some years back. And I've found her current home address, in Silverlake Forest."

"She's been at the Tamarack News for three years, according to their website," May said. "And her previous experience was in New York. That seems to be where she went to school, from what I can see here."

"Perhaps she connected with the Reeds there?" Owen said. "They have a lot of business interests in New York."

May nodded. "It could well be. Were they ever friends of hers, I wonder? Did things go wrong? How well does she really know them?"

"I'll see what I can find out about Emily's social connections," Owen said. "You want to do the same?"

Turning to her laptop, May changed her browser to access social media.

"Now this is interesting," she said. "Look here, Owen."

"What?" he asked, leaning over.

"Emily dated Danny Charter a couple of years ago!"

May couldn't believe her eyes. There was the connection they'd been seeking. Clearer and closer than she'd expected.

Just eighteen months ago, they'd been a couple. The photos were there to prove it. They'd gone to dinner together. Gone to movies together. Been a good-looking pair at parties. Emily's delicate blond looks were a good foil for Danny's solid dark-haired charm.

Now, Danny, whom Emily had been dating, was murdered and Madeline, whom Emily likely had been blackmailing, was murdered.

They had finally found the common thread they needed. Now the pieces were falling into place.

"What's her address?" May said, feeling elated at the breakthrough they'd just made. We need to drive there immediately! Let's get my car."

Remembering her car was with Kerry, she quickly amended, "Your car, if that's okay, Owen."

*

Ten minutes later, May and Owen were speeding along the main road to Silverlake Forest, where Emily's residential address was located.

Speaking out loud, May listed the facts she'd assembled in her mind.

"So this entire scenario could have been blackmail gone wrong," she said.

"How so?" Quickly, Owen overtook two slower moving cars before veering back into his lane.

"Let's assume that Madeline Reed was bringing in labor on the cheap from Eastern Europe, during those recruitment trips, and that they were cutting corners somewhere along the way to save on costs. Most likely, the workers might be treated badly, underpaid, their visas not in correct order," May hazarded.

"Right. I'm assuming that."

"Emily must have found out about all of this. Perhaps Danny clued her in on Madeline's role. Maybe he was going to take a cut. She then blackmailed Madeline, who paid her to keep quiet."

"Then what do you think happened?" Owen sped the car around a sharp corner, tires wailing.

"Perhaps Danny got greedy. He wanted more than what Emily was prepared to pay him. So she killed him. And perhaps Madeline started getting ugly and threatening her. Maybe Madeline found out who she was and threatened to expose her. There are lots of potential scenarios and reasons. So she killed her, too."

"That would make sense," Owen said. "Sort of, I guess. I guess it all hinges on how badly Madeline wanted to protect her reputation, and how illegal her cheap labor was."

"I'm sure Emily must have done research on that," May said.

They had reached the town where Emily lived. Now they were accelerating to its outskirts. May felt herself growing nervous. They were about to confront a woman who they suspected of committing two violent murders. There was no telling what might play out when they banged on her front door.

"Let's come up with a plan," May said. "That way we're ready for whatever happens."

"Good idea."

"We need to start by demanding to see her bank account. That will tell us a lot."

"But we need to make sure she doesn't pull a weapon, make a run for it, something like that. From the minute we get in there, we need to be alert and on the defensive."

It was a sobering thought. They were about to confront a woman for two murders. If she were to attack them, they would be forced to defend themselves.

"Yes. We must be on our guard," May agreed.

"We must also record everything she says if she starts to confess," Owen said.

"Good idea," May said. "I have my phone with me."

"And I have my tablet," Owen said. He reached into his jacket pocket and pulled out the device.

"Good." May's heart was racing. Everything was happening fast. "I don't think we'll need to use our guns, though. I hope we don't."

"Me too," Owen said.

"Here we are," May said. "This is her road. Her house is number five."

The house was small but well kept. In the dusk, May could see it had a great view of the lake behind it. A spectacular sunset was brightening the sky in shades of amber, rust, and gold.

"This is the place," she said, letting out a long breath.

"Looks quiet. Let's go up and knock," Owen said.

They parked the car in front of Emily's house and walked up to the front door. Adrenaline surged inside her. She couldn't wait to confront this strong suspect, who had a motive for both murders. Was she home?

May could see a light on in the window. She hoped that meant Emily was home. But her heart started beating faster as she approached the front door.

It wasn't locked. It wasn't even fully closed. It was standing ajar, with a beam of faint light filtering out.

"What's going on here? This isn't right," Owen whispered.

"No, it isn't," she agreed, as they slowed down and looked at each other. Worst-case scenarios were flooding May's mind. She didn't want to think about the reason for that partly open door.

May stepped up to the door and knocked hard, peeking through the gap as she did.

"Emily Oxman!" she called. "Are you inside?"

There was no answer. The house was quiet. The light was on in the hall, but it didn't look to be disturbed. Nothing was knocked over or lying around.

With a sinking sensation, May was starting to suspect the worst. What if someone else had come for Emily, to get their revenge?

Looking at Owen, she could see he shared this exact fear. He tiptoed around to the closest window.

"I can't see anything in the lounge," he reported in a whisper. Moving further around the house, he added, "And the garage door is open, with no car inside."

May pushed the front door wider and walked inside. She had to know if this woman was lying dead inside her house, or not.

The curtains were still open in the bedroom, she saw. Some clothes lay on the bed, which was neatly made. The wardrobe door was open, and one of the drawers on the dressing table was, too. Otherwise, there was no sign of disturbance in the small room, or in the kitchen, or in the bathroom as she hurried from room to room, checking. No toothbrush in the bathroom. That was gone.

She walked outside again and met Owen there.

"I've checked the yard. Nothing's out of place," he reported.

"I think she's fled," May concluded. "This doesn't seem like a burglary. There's no sign of a struggle and no sign of her car. It looks like she packed some clothes in the bedroom, took what she needed, and left. I think she knew we'd suspect she did it, and she's done a runner."

It was a clear sign of her guilt. But she had the jump on them, and they were lagging behind.

Their strong suspect had gotten away, and now they would have to hunt her down.

CHAPTER SIXTEEN

At nine p.m. May and Owen pulled up outside the home of the *Tamarack News* financial editor, Adele Wong.

May hoped Adele might have some answers, because so far they'd come up with nothing. They'd coordinated an intensive search of the wider area. A roadblock was still operational on the route to the highway. Sheriff Jack had put out the APB on Emily's vehicle, liaising with police in other counties as far as the state border.

Feeling tired and discouraged, May walked up to the front door of the pretty home on the edge of the woods in Misty Hills. She knocked on the door, wondering if by some miracle they would find Emily sheltering here.

A few moments later, Adele opened the door. The dark-haired woman was dressed casually in jeans and a sweater, and looked extremely surprised to see them standing there.

"Good evening. Has anything happened?" she asked curiously.

"We're looking for Emily Oxman."

Now Adele looked shocked.

"Why? Is it something to do with that piece we published?"

"No. It's other reasons," May said. "We went to her home and found she had already left, leaving it open. She hasn't been back. It is looking suspicious and we need to find her urgently. Do you have any idea where she could be?"

"I don't know. I know she has quite a few friends in Tamarack County. Journalists are always well connected. But unfortunately I wouldn't know who her closest friends are. Her family is in New York State, that I do know."

"Did she leave the office much today? You mentioned she was out earlier?" May asked, wanting to confirm if the timeline of Emily's movements would have allowed for her to visit the Rushway River Lodge."

Adele sighed. "She wasn't in the office at all today," she said.

"Not at all?" May's eyes widened.

"No. She often takes days out, or half days out, if she's researching a story. It was not unusual that she didn't come in. However, I also didn't ask her where she was, as I had meetings throughout the day. And nor did she tell me, I'm afraid."

Her absence from the office meant she could have had the chance to kill Madeline. May felt highly suspicious that she'd been out and about all day.

"If she messages you, please try to find out where she is," May said. "And please don't tell her we were here. That needs to remain confidential, as this is a murder investigation."

"I won't say a word to her," Adele promised, looking serious and stressed as they turned away.

Climbing back in the car, May felt tired and frustrated.

"How can there be no sign of her?" she asked Owen as he headed back to the police department. "How can she just have disappeared?"

"She's probably hidden herself away in a remote location, or holed up with one of her friends," Owen suggested. "If she was driving out on the road, we would have found her by now. With the APB and the roadblocks and our own search, we did everything we could."

"I'm worried that she's left the state," May said. "If she's done a runner, she could be anywhere by now. That's very bad news."

With tiredness and discouragement warring inside her, May was forced to face her limitations as a small-town cop again.

The FBI would have more resources at their disposal, she knew. They would be able to pour far more into the hunt, access more personnel and equipment, and even track Emily's phone.

May tried to console herself by thinking that if Emily was in hiding, and had turned off her phone, then not even the FBI would be able to find her. But even so, she couldn't help feeling a sense of helplessness. They had pinned down their prime suspect and she was out of reach.

Owen gave her a sympathetic glance.

"We did our best," he said. "You can't beat yourself up. There's nothing more we could have done."

"I know. I know you're right." But she felt defeated as they pulled up outside the Fairshore police department.

"Come on, we'll tell Jack the latest," Owen said. "Maybe he'll have some good news."

"I'm sure he would have called us if there was any news," May said, not wanting to get her hopes up.

She headed into the police department wondering what else they could possibly do to track Emily down.

Inside the back office, Sheriff Jack was busy on the radio. Her boss gave them a warm, if tired, smile.

"Evening, May and Owen. I've just been in touch with everyone again and there's still no sign of her or her vehicle anywhere."

He rubbed a hand across the back of his neck.

"If only we could find her," May said, feeling weary. She slumped into a chair.

"I can't see how she could have driven across the state line without anyone picking her up," Jack said reassuringly.

May nodded, but couldn't help feeling a sense of frustration. She was tired and worried. They had a murderer on the loose, and it was her job to catch her.

"It's still good work on your part, May," Jack said. "This is a very solid lead. You've done a great job getting this far in such a short time."

He looked at her and she sensed that he was trying to reassure her. She appreciated it, but it didn't make her feel much better.

The stress and activity of the evening was reminding her of that awful day ten years ago when Lauren had disappeared. There had been the same searches, the same activity, the same peaks of hope as leads were followed, which had ended in crashes of disappointment as they didn't pan out.

May thought again of that evidence box, stashed away in the back office. If only she'd looked inside. If only she had more of a clue about Lauren.

Thinking about Lauren gave her a sudden idea about Emily.

"The airports, Jack. Have they all been told to watch out for her? She could easily have dumped the car somewhere and then taken a cab. She could be planning to fly out of here, to another state or even another country."

"Yes, they have. All security teams at all the airports are aware she's a person of interest and they must seize her if they find her. And I've stationed an officer outside her house for the night, so we'll know immediately if she comes back or sends anyone else to her home."

"Is there anything else we can do? Anything?" May asked.

Jack shook his head. "I'm about to wrap up operations here for the night. We've done what we can. We all need to keep our phones on so we can react immediately if we do get a notification, but for now, we need to get some rest and start again in the morning."

May and Owen headed outside. The evening was warm, with a pleasant breeze. The town was quiet and peaceful.

It was hard to believe that just a few hours ago they'd been accelerating along these same streets, on their way to the home of the person they suspected to be the killer. If only they could have gotten there earlier, they might have been in time to stop her.

She felt a sense of disappointment and frustration. They had come so close to catching Emily, only to have her slip through their fingers.

"Come on, May. Let's get home. I'm sure she's hiding away for the night, and will make a move tomorrow morning," Owen said, in an encouraging voice. "It's better we're rested for her then. We won't get anywhere sitting here overnight, with nothing to do except worry."

They really couldn't do more. They'd exhausted every avenue. Finally, with a sigh, May capitulated and accepted this.

She climbed into Owen's car and he headed out into the dark, quiet streets. At this time of night, May's house was only a four-minute drive away.

She lived on the far side of town, away from the lake. Knowing her sister had disappeared on those shores, May hadn't wanted to stare out at those waters every day.

She lived in a cottage next to a farmhouse. It was quiet and peaceful, and her view was of fields and trees.

"Thank you so much for the ride," she told Owen as he approached the small, homely cottage.

For a weird moment, May suddenly wondered if she should ask her deputy to come in for a cup of coffee.

It seemed like a friendly thing to do. After all, they'd worked together the whole day. They'd chased and strategized and planned together. She suddenly realized how much she appreciated Owen's company. He was a tower of strength.

But then at the last minute she decided against the coffee. It was very late, after all. And what if Owen got the wrong idea and it all became awkward?

Wondering what the right idea was, and what that coffee might have meant to her, May got out of the car and headed inside.

She was looking forward to getting some sleep, but as she climbed into bed, her phone beeped. It was Kerry.

Her heart accelerated when she saw the message. Was this about the case? Was her sister still pushing to be involved?

Feeling extremely nervous, May opened the message.

"Hi, sis! Brandon's getting here very early tomorrow. We've organized an early breakfast at the folks', and you're invited! I'll pick you up on the way back from the airport at around seven a.m. See you then!"

May's heart plummeted.

She didn't know if she would be able to attend this breakfast. It all depended on what happened with the case.

But if she was able to, May had no doubt that it would be a trying experience in every way, one to be endured rather than enjoyed, because it would target all her own insecurities.

She hoped to goodness that Emily made her move by tomorrow morning. Not only would it progress the case, but it would allow her to skip an event she was already dreading.

CHAPTER SEVENTEEN

As soon as May woke up after a restless sleep, she grabbed her phone, hoping for an update on the case. But her phone was stubbornly silent. It was six-thirty a.m. and she had half an hour before Kerry and Brandon arrived.

With a sigh, May got out of bed and jumped in the shower. She interrupted her shower twice to check her phone, feeling nervous and jumpy and anxious that at any moment, the call might come through that she needed.

But there was no call.

She dried her hair and put on some make-up and got dressed and checked her phone again. And then she stood outside, waiting for Kerry to arrive and hoping that her pickup had survived the ride.

As she looked up and down the street, she felt a little pang of disappointment. It was such a beautiful morning. The air was fresh and the sun was just peeking over the horizon, brightening a cloudless summer sky. And here she was, about to step into what was certain to be a challenging family event.

"What a way to start my day," she said out loud, but nobody heard, because she was completely alone.

The street was silent and empty, but then, from the main road, she heard the sound of a fast-revving engine. She saw her pickup—thankfully undamaged—swerve into the street and brake sharply in front of her house.

Kerry was at the wheel. Riding next to her was a handsome, dark-haired man wearing a business suit.

"Morning," Kerry said, grinning at her. "Meet Brandon. Brandon, this is my little sister May."

"Great to meet you." Turning as she climbed into the car, Brandon gave her a flashing, hundred-watt smile. He looked successful and strong, but as he maintained eye contact, she got the impression he was kind and caring. What else could she have expected from Kerry's beau? Of course he would be without flaws!

"Pleased to meet you," May said, trying to sound as enthusiastic as she could.

Taking a deep breath, she sat back and held on for dear life.

Kerry revved the engine and then let out the clutch. Spinning the wheel, she pulled away from the curb. The pickup accelerated down the street and then onto the main road.

She was used to her sister's love of speed. Kerry raced through the streets of Fairshore with her foot hard against the pedal. The pickup screeched around a corner, and then suddenly the brakes were on and they came to a shuddering halt outside their folks' place.

May had wondered if Kerry would mention the case, or ask if May had made progress, but she had been too focused on her driving. At least that was a small benefit, May thought, with a sense of irony.

The front door of the house was open and her parents were standing there. Getting out of the car, May could already smell the aromas of cooking food.

She knew the breakfast spread would be perfect, and the table immaculately prepared. That was how her mother did things.

"Oh, Kerry!" Her mother was wearing her best red suit, the one she wore to weddings and big events. "This is such an exciting day for us. I can't believe that we're meeting your fiancé. Your fiancé! What an incredible moment this is."

"Good morning, Mr. and Mrs. Moore," Brandon said, striding across the sidewalk and shaking hands with May's mother. "It's so wonderful to finally meet you!"

"Welcome to our family!" May's mother enthused. "I'm excited to hear your wedding plans."

"It's going to be a very special day," he said. "I'll be making a promise to the woman of my dreams. I feel very privileged to be marrying into your family."

May's dad shook his hand.

"It's a real pleasure to meet you, sir," Brandon said, giving her dad a firm grip. Then Brandon put his arms around Kerry and kissed her gently on the lips.

May waited for someone, anyone, to greet her. She knew all the focus was on Kerry and that this was a very special and important day. But why, oh why, did her parents not see her the same way? In fact, with their attention on Kerry, why did they not see her at all?

Briefly, she wished Lauren was still here. Imagine if she and Lauren could smile at each other at this moment, both sharing the same thoughts and emotions, both pleased for Kerry but resigned over the level of fuss that this event triggered.

May missed her other sister intensely right at that moment.

They went inside. The house was every inch as clean and neat as May had expected it to be. There were fresh flowers in the hallway and the living room was immaculate, with every cushion perfectly plumped.

"Make yourself at home," her father said, leading them into the dining room. "Lovely to see both of you here."

"It's wonderful to have both my daughters at our table again," her mother agreed.

The table was set with a white tablecloth and her mother's good china, and the food was laid out, ready to be served. It was an impressive spread.

The smell of bacon and eggs, sausages, and grilled tomatoes filled the air. There was homemade bread and croissants, mushrooms and cornbread, Danish pastries, and a huge pot of coffee.

"Mom, you didn't have to go to all this effort," Kerry said. "This is an absolute feast!"

"I wanted to. It's so exciting to have a new member of the family," she said, a proud smile on her face.

"So, Brandon, have you decided on a destination for the honeymoon?" May's father asked.

"We're going to the Maldives. We'll be spending a week at a top resort, adventuring around the area."

"Oh, how wonderful!" May's mother exclaimed.

"I've always wanted to go there," May's father said. "I hear it's gorgeous."

"I've dreamed of going to the Maldives for as long as I can remember," Kerry said. "I can't wait to get there. I have always thought it's the most romantic destination."

"But what about your wedding? First things first," her mother said. "Let's get the food on the plates and you can tell me what you have planned. What can I dish up for you, Brandon? Mushrooms? Cornbread? You'll have bacon, of course?"

"Everything looks delicious," Brandon said.

"And for you, dear?" her mother said, turning to Kerry.

"I'll have the eggs, and give me plenty of bacon."

"And for you, May?"

Those were the first words her mother had spoken to her directly, and what was worse, she didn't even seem to notice.

"A bit of everything, please." She smiled, determined to contribute positive energy to this important breakfast.

"There you go, honey. It means so much to me that you're here for such an important event," her mother enthused, passing the plate to her.

May couldn't help thinking of Lauren again. One day they had been three, and then two. She felt suddenly sad. If only Lauren could have been here too. Wasn't anyone else missing her?

"We're planning on a spring wedding, but that actually doesn't give us long to get everything figured out," Brandon said. "What we visualize is to have the ceremony outdoors, in a little glade."

"Oh, that sounds wonderful. It's going to be so unique," her mother said.

"It will be lovely," Kerry said.

"I can't wait to see your wedding dress. Have you decided on a theme?"

"We thought we'd go with a classic look," Kerry said. "Nothing too fussy. I want silver and white as the décor theme."

"Oh, my dear, I'm sure you'll look just beautiful," her mother said.

"Brandon, do you want more bacon?" May's father asked. "It's the best in town."

"I've never been a part of a family like this," Brandon said. "You've been so welcoming. It's amazing."

At that moment, May's phone rang. She jumped, grabbing it from her pocket. It was Jack on the line.

"I'm sorry. I have to take this. I may have to rush away. Thank you so much for a wonderful meal," she said. Grabbing her purse, she hurried out of the dining room, feeling relieved to have a reason for leaving the table.

"May. We have some news." Jack sounded excited.

"What's happened?" she asked.

"Emily's been found. She arrived at a small local airport about an hour ago. Airport security picked her up and arrested her, and she's on the way to the police department. You need to come in as soon as possible so that we can question her."

Suddenly, May felt as if this day, which had started so awkwardly, was full of hope and promise.

Their strong suspect was on the way in. Soon, this case might be closed.

"I'll be there in five minutes," she said.

The keys to the pickup were on the hall table. Her pickup. Kerry didn't need it anymore. She could use her folks' car for getting around town.

Grabbing the keys, May called out a quick goodbye to the family. She wasn't sure if anyone heard her.

She rushed out to the car, climbed inside, and sped off to the police department, her mind filled with the make or break interview ahead.

CHAPTER EIGHTEEN

May pulled up outside the police department feeling hopeful, as if the investigation was finally starting to turn her way.

And she had her wheels back, undamaged and her own again.

Owen arrived a moment after she did. They exchanged a quick, excited glance before rushing in. Despite the early hour, the police department was a hive of activity. Two of the security staff from the airport were still on site. So Emily Oxman must have just arrived.

May felt nervous at the thought of questioning her. This was going to be a huge opportunity, questioning a strong suspect in a murder case. She hoped she'd be able to get the right answers from this woman. She guessed Jack would take the lead, but she hoped she'd be able to give some input.

Jack bustled out of the room a moment later.

"Right," he said. "Good morning, team. Everything is set up and ready. May, you can handle this interview, together with Owen. I'll step in if you need me, or if you want a different person asking questions."

"Me?" May asked.

She felt astonished by this display of trust and confidence from her boss.

"You worked out the link between the victim and the suspect, and then you did the research we needed. You've handled this case superbly every step of the way, and you need to manage this next step."

"Are you sure?" she asked.

"You'll be fine. You're good at this. Just follow your instincts and your gut feeling."

Feeling cheered by her boss's praise, May rushed to the back office to get her notebook.

"Shall we go in?" she asked Owen.

"I'm ready," he agreed.

Taking a deep breath, May stepped into the interview room and came face to face for the first time with her prime suspect.

The slim, blond woman stared back at her. Something about her expression, the defiant set of her jaw, made May instantly wary.

Emily didn't look the type to be easily intimidated. She looked like she'd been around the block a few times and knew exactly how to handle herself. She didn't look like someone who'd easily succumb to pressure or threats.

May knew she had only moments to read this woman and decide on an approach.

She told herself firmly, as she sat, that there was no need for her to be intimidated by this woman. She had the law on her side. She had an entire police department behind her. This woman was their suspect for very strong reasons, and they'd interrogate her until they got answers.

May sat down and stared at Emily silently. She wanted her to feel uncomfortable with the silence. She wanted her to start fearing what May might say. That would be the best approach, she thought.

May let it build, noting Emily's reaction.

She was heartened to see Emily shift in her seat, trying to make herself more comfortable. Suddenly, she looked a little more nervous, as if being alone with her thoughts hadn't gone well for her.

It felt like a game of cat and mouse, a game where May hoped she'd get to be the cat and Emily the mouse.

"I'm going to record this interview," she said at last. She pressed the recording button on the machine.

"Please state your full name," she said.

"Emily Ruth Oxman," the journalist replied in a soft voice.

"Ms. Oxman, I'd like to remind you that this is a criminal investigation. Failure to comply with questioning, lying while being questioned, or not telling the full truth may count against you."

"I understand," Emily replied. Her voice was calm and strong but May saw her face twitch.

"I'm going to give you the chance to tell me this information of your own free will, before we seize the records ourselves," May said firmly.

She saw Emily's eyes narrow at that.

"Have you received any recent payments into your bank account from anyone connected with the Reed family?" May asked.

Emily stared at her in utter shock. She'd turned sheet white. Clearly, she had not expected this question at all, still less as the starting point. It had thrown her completely.

May guessed she was floored that they'd found out, and inwardly she felt deeply thankful to Kerry for providing the vital research she needed.

86

"I have the right to remain silent, I believe," Emily said defiantly, her voice shaking.

"You may have the right to remain silent, but the law assumes you'll tell the truth," May said. "You may be in a position to make things easier for yourself if you do so. Denying that this payment was made will go very badly for you when we present the proof to the jury."

The mention of the criminal trial in her future caused Emily to flinch.

"I didn't do it," she said in a shaking voice.

"Didn't do what?" May said. She glanced at Owen and saw him briefly narrow his eyes. It was definitely the interview room equivalent of a high five. They were getting somewhere.

"I know you've brought me in because of the two murders. I know you suspect me. But I didn't do it!"

"I don't believe we're at that point. We are still discussing the payment into your account," May said firmly.

Emily let out a deep breath. She shook her head hard.

"Tell us about it," May said.

"I—well, I guess—look, it's not like you think. Danny put me up to this. He never liked her. Never liked Madeline."

"Put you up to what?" May asked, curious to hear more.

Emily fidgeted in her seat, as if fighting her desire to run and hide.

"The money—the five hundred thousand dollars—it was supposed to be divided between Danny and me."

"How did you extort it?"

"Danny wrote the letter and sent it. He used an anonymous email account. But he then provided my bank details. Because obviously he couldn't use his own details, and my bank account is in my married name, which I don't use anymore. Emily Brown. He said she'd never work out who that was, and if she did, she would be too scared to retaliate and that I didn't need to worry."

"And why?"

Emily made a face. "Look, it had to do with the Eastern European workers. There were irregularities there. I received a tip-off, anonymously, a couple of weeks ago, and I was planning on researching it for an article, but when I mentioned this to Danny, he came up with the blackmail idea as a better option. He said we should just do the demand, and not have the media digging into it. And because he was my ex, and I'd already written one incriminating article on the hotel because my boss told me to, and he sort of persuaded me, I left it at that."

May's eyebrows rose upon hearing that.

"Why did Danny say that?" she asked.

"Look, I don't fully know what the issue was. I was a fool to go along with it. Danny can be very persuasive. But like I said, I didn't write the email! Danny handled that side. He didn't want me involved, and he wanted a complete circuit-breaker, as he called it, between the demand for money and the bank account."

"And you were going to split it?"

"That's right."

"But then Danny died?"

Emily spread her arms. "I was devastated about that. I still am. We used to date a couple of years ago. You probably know that because I can see you have done your research. We were still good friends. I thought he was a wild kid, and I shouldn't have gone along with that proposal, but I did."

"Do you have an alibi for that evening?" May asked. "What were your movements on the night he died?"

"The night before last?" She made a face. "This is not going to sound good, I know. I met with Danny."

"Tell us about that."

"We met up at a bar near the hotel. It was nothing, really, just a friendly chat."

But something in the way she mumbled the words made May think it had been more.

"Name the bar," May said sternly. "Remember, we need a full account from you, and we may already know a lot of the information from other sources."

Emily sighed, looking defeated. "It was the Bellevue Bar."

"And what happened between you there?" May glared at her.

Emily looked down. "I'd just received the payment. And we argued about it. We had a fight. He wanted more of the money than we'd agreed. He started threatening that he'd tell Madeline who I was, and that I was an idiot, and that he'd really just engineered the whole thing to stop me from writing the article because it wouldn't be good for the business to have it written. And that now my career was over and he would make sure I was destroyed. We ended up shouting at each other. It got so bad the bartender came over to ask what was wrong. He heard most of it. You probably know this already. Then he stormed out. I stayed and had another glass of wine, and then left."

May couldn't believe what she was hearing. This gave Emily an extreme, urgent motive for the murders.

"Any proof of when you left?" May asked.

She shook her head. "I don't remember. But it wasn't more than half an hour after he left."

"And yesterday afternoon?"

Now Emily shook her head.

"I wasn't with anyone. I was home alone. Look, I need my lawyer. I really need my lawyer. I can't keep answering this way. I don't have an alibi. I never thought I'd need one. I promise you. I didn't do it."

"Why did you run then?" Owen asked.

Emily let out a frustrated sigh.

"Because I knew that after what played out, and our argument, and the murders, it was extremely likely that the police would catch up with me and find that damned money in my account. Blackmail's a felony, I am aware of that. I was involved in blackmail and now it looks like I'm a murderer, too. When I heard Madeline was dead, I knew how people would think. I'm a journalist. I see these stories all the time. I literally don't know what to say here."

She stared at May with desperation in her eyes. May saw she was about to cry. Her eyes were swimming with tears.

"We'll be back," May said. She got up and walked out.

Outside, Jack and one of the other officers who had been listening in the adjoining room were high-fiving each other.

"You got great answers out of her, May. I think we have enough to build a solid case," Jack praised her. "What a stroke of luck you asked her about the bar. That will add a lot to the evidence."

"Congratulations. You did awesomely. I didn't think you'd break her, but you went right in and found her weak points," Owen said.

May felt warm inside and grateful for their words of commendation. But inside, she couldn't help feeling a creeping sense of doubt.

Was it just her own insecurity raising its head? she wondered with a chill.

Or were there really holes in this seemingly solid case that might come back to bite her at a later stage, when too much time had passed to find out the truth? After all, Emily hadn't actually confessed. She'd said she had no alibi and she'd admitted to the blackmail. But she'd begged them to believe she wasn't the killer, and the look in her eyes had seemed genuine and truthful.

May decided she wasn't going to let even a moment's negligence compromise the case. She couldn't bear the thought of the wrong person being arrested or, worse still, the case going cold.

Whatever it took, she was going to try and fill the gaps in Emily's story now. And she had a good idea where to start. It might be only a tiny gap she saw, but it was troubling her.

CHAPTER NINETEEN

The killer knew who the next target was. A man who deserved to die just as much as the others. A terrible man, whose day of reckoning had finally come. He was the hotel's personnel manager. He carried a burden of guilt. He was a criminal and a thief.

There he was. After a patient couple of days of waiting and stalking, this man was finally where he needed to be.

He'd been doing the staffing register at the hotel's liquor warehouse, where the casual workers had just been paid.

He was alone now. A thickset man with spiky hair that stood off his scalp like he'd been electrocuted. Narrow, unpleasant eyes. Big hands.

A strong man, but the killer hoped he was not a fast man, or a suspicious person. At any rate, he was not expecting anyone to be following him. He was expecting to go about his business alone, as he always did.

Except he wasn't. Not this afternoon.

The killer watched him with pleasure and anticipation, knowing that soon this man would be dead.

But not yet. The killer had a special plan for this man.

Now he was pacing the aisle of the warehouse. The killer knew this warehouse was used as a central point by a few of the company's hotels. Although a busy place, it was seldom guarded, and once you were through the main door, there was no shortage of cover.

The killer followed the manager, staying in the shadows at first. Getting a feel for the space and the man.

It was a noisy, poorly lit, clanging area. The bulky piles of boxes provided cover and hiding places. Shelves lined the walls and bisected the space between.

The draft beer was transported in large barrels. Barrels that were large enough to hold a man's head under while he drowned.

The killer was waiting patiently for him to go where he needed to be, into the small temporary office which he used to write up his records. The casual workers were paid in cash and the killer was sure that he skimmed some off, so that they lost and he won. That was the way he worked.

It would be the perfect time to make sure this miserable life was snuffed out.

The killer watched the manager pace between the stacks of boxes. A big, swaggering man, who thought he was hiding his sins.

The killer smiled. The manager had a lot to learn. He was convincing no one.

But the killer knew. And the killer would make him pay.

This man didn't deserve to live after what he had done. He was the personification of the rottenness that lurked beneath the shiny, polished exterior of this hotel. That wasn't only because he skimmed money from poor people who needed their wages.

Recently, the killer knew, the manager had gotten into a fight over a woman.

The man he'd fought with was already dead. Danny had died in the lake. Now it was the manager's turn. The fight had been over a woman, that was true, but the full truth ran much deeper, an ugly seam that was hidden under the hotel's shiny veneer. The truth was that they were both enablers. Both users.

It was the killer's job to expose this seam. To punish the people involved. And to leave the message that was also the ultimate humiliation. The five-dollar bill stuffed into their throats.

Take that! Take that and let people remember forever what you did!

The killer followed him for a while, enjoying the way the manager took the time to glance around arrogantly, like he was someone to be feared.

Well, he was, the killer thought with a smile. But not for the reasons he thought.

The killer looked around. The warehouse was empty now. There was no movement in the distance. No sound. It was always a busier place in the morning. By late afternoon it was quiet, the orders fulfilled, the boxes moved to their destinations where the evening trade would begin. The workers paid and gone.

But now, it was necessary to be patient just a little longer.

The killer had thought that a wine bottle would be the best weapon to use, but a gleam of metal showed the way to an even better one.

In this busy warehouse, with its shelves and equipment and machinery, someone had left a metal wrench on the bottom shelf, near an open box of whiskey bottles. That would work perfectly. And it would not shatter.

Now the only thing that was needed was for the manager to go where he needed to be, where he would be sitting down with his back turned, perfectly positioned for the first stage of the kill.

The beer barrels were just outside the office and the killer felt confident that this semi-conscious man could easily be dragged to the heavy, waist-high vats once the deed was done. It would be a great pleasure to put him in the barrel.

It would be like drowning a rat.

The killer watched.

The manager had stopped pacing. He was looking around, as if expecting to see someone.

Quickly, the killer ducked out of sight. What was going on? The man was looking furtive now, his earlier confidence gone. The killer saw the manager's face. It was creased in concentration, his brow furrowed as he touched the pockets of his jacket. Whatever he was looking for, he wasn't finding.

And then the manager reached into his pants pocket and shook out a joint. The killer watched as he lit it and inhaled deeply.

The manager was high and that was good. It would make things easier. What a loser, taking drugs on the job. Just another indication of who he really was, as soon as everyone's back was turned.

The killer smiled, preparing to go into action.

It would be a simple job once the first part was done. Then the second stage could begin.

The killer's heart beat faster, thinking about it. It was all coming together beautifully. What a pleasure it would be to turn the tables on this man.

The killer followed him, staying in the shadows. Turning a corner, the manager shambled toward the small office. The killer was close behind.

The manager was strolling along, unworried. A little high, but not suspicious. Maybe he was thinking of the girl. But she was nothing to him. His squeeze toy. A means to an end. It was a violation. And that's what he was. A violator.

Rage surged in the killer at the unfairness of the situation. There was only one way to make it right and it needed to be done.

The manager stopped by the beer barrels, tapping his fingers on the tops of the drums. He did it in an absent way, a distracted way.

Four yellow tops. Perfect. The man didn't even notice that one was already loosened and ready. He wasn't thinking of his job. Why would he? He was not that caliber of man. He was getting high, and most likely thinking of the woman.

Only she was not his, and never would be. And in a few more minutes, he would never see her again.

He stood there, his back turned, smoking his joint. Then, satisfied that all was as it should be, he turned to the door and went inside.

Soon, the killer thought. Soon.

The manager sat down heavily at the desk and pulled out the forms he needed for his records.

He reached for a pen, took a swig of his coffee, then he began to tap on his laptop and write on the forms. In the quietness of the warehouse, the rattle of the keyboard and the scratching of the pen on paper sounded loud.

Gripping the wrench tightly, the killer smiled.

CHAPTER TWENTY

May felt utterly conflicted. She walked outside, pacing up and down, her shadow sharp on the sidewalk in the bright afternoon sun. She was wishing she was more at peace with the suspect everyone else seemed to think represented a slam-dunk case.

But May didn't.

Sighing, she turned and paced the other way, hoping that the regular movement would bring some clarity to her thoughts and allow her to understand why she felt this way.

Emily had a strong motive. She had no alibi. She'd fought with Danny over the money and he'd threatened to expose her to Madeline and destroy her.

It couldn't point back to her more clearly—and yet, May doubted her guilt.

For a start, a journalist who had been cunning and wicked enough to preplan these murders would either have concocted herself a strong alibi, or else escaped the state, or even the country, sooner. Right after the second murder would have been the time to flee. If she'd done that she would have been free and clear, far beyond the reach of the Tamarack County police, and even beyond the FBI, if she'd chosen her destination carefully.

But she hadn't. She'd waited, and then panicked and run, then hid, and then arrived at a local airport the next morning.

Was that because she hadn't known about the second murder soon enough? Because to May, that sequence of events looked like the actions of someone who hadn't known about the murder and when she had found out, feared that she would be the suspect.

And she'd seemed so traumatized. So distraught. So genuinely scared.

May just couldn't work out how that mindset aligned with a killer who had been ice cold enough to hit two people over the head, hold them under water to drown them, and then stuff a five-dollar bill into their throat.

Looking around, she saw Owen was standing at the entrance door and staring at her curiously.

He moved aside to let a member of the public through, and then walked out to join May.

"Are you okay?" he said. "Are you feeling bad about her being arrested?"

"I'm feeling worried about having made a mistake," May admitted.

"You have to believe in your instincts," Owen told her. "Otherwise, you're just an officer taking orders. So if your instincts are telling you something, I'm sure there's a reason for it."

"I'm just not able to think what the reason is," May said.

"It's difficult to work out because it's such a cut and dried case, isn't it?" Owen asked. "All the evidence is pointing to her. I mean, it couldn't be more clear cut. It's like a rock solid chain of proof."

"Why didn't Emily run earlier? She could have fled the country long before we worked out she was the common thread."

Owen shrugged. "Criminals aren't always the most intelligent."

"But she seems like an intelligent person. And she had the money to do it."

"Then maybe it's reverse psychology," he suggested. "Trying to make you think she didn't do it?"

May sighed.

"Why did she confess to the blackmail but not the murder?"

"Well, they're very different levels of offense. Plus, she wasn't that involved in the blackmail demand, was she?" Owen reasoned. "It was more from Danny's side. She was just the recipient of the funds."

May stared at Owen.

"You just said something important there!"

"I did?" Owen looked startled.

"Yes. You reminded me about her role in that blackmail. That's actually one of the things that was worrying me."

"What was?"

Now Owen was pacing up and down, in step with her.

"The reason for the blackmail."

"How do you mean?"

"It didn't make total sense to me. That's a lot of money to pay."

"Yes," Owen said, looking serious. "It was a huge amount."

"I'm not sure the reason is good enough. Paying such a massive sum in blackmail because you're cutting corners by employing a few people without the right papers to work for less just doesn't make sense. I know the penalties for doing that are harsh but they have the best lawyers. And from what she told us, Danny didn't want her to go digging. He engineered the whole thing to manipulate her so that she couldn't."

"Yes. You're right. I also wondered if there was more to that, but since Danny and Madeline were both killed, I felt we'd never know. Perhaps it doesn't matter, though? Do you think the details are important? Surely what she said paves the way to the truth?"

May shook her head.

"I'm worried there's more. And that maybe we should be doing the digging now."

They both turned and paced the other way. May felt hugely grateful for Owen's support. He wasn't shouting her down or telling her she was wrong. Instead, he was supporting her and respecting that she had doubts.

She felt incredibly lucky to have a partner who was able to offer so much empathy, and who was also not afraid to relook at a case with the possibility that they'd made a mistake.

"There's something we're missing. Something that's sitting right in front of us, but we're just not seeing it."

May knew that very well. She knew how it felt to be so close to the answer but not see it. It was a horrible feeling. A feeling of powerlessness.

"So, what details do we know then? Where can we start? Perhaps we can look at what we know for sure, and then work out the bigger picture based on that?" Owen asked.

"They definitely do employ Eastern European workers at the hotel. So that's correct. And Madeline definitely traveled to that country frequently, according to the law firm."

"I remember that maid who served us tea. Her accent was definitely from that part of the world." Owen nodded.

"I know she was terrified of something. And when she came in, the guard was leering at her."

May remembered that woman clearly. She remembered the fear in her eyes as she'd brought in the tea. And most definitely, the way that the guard had ogled her had been out of line.

It had almost seemed as if she was just a thing, rather than a human being. That was what May had picked up. It had made her feel very uneasy, she remembered. She'd been about to mention it and say something angry, because she wasn't the type to keep quiet, but then someone else had said something, and the maid had left the room, and she'd gotten sidetracked.

Now, she was wishing she'd spoken up because it might have somehow helped her understand what was really happening. If only she'd said something then, she might know more now.

She was wishing she had listened to her instincts and engaged with the maid.

"Yes. It's terrible that this hotel seems to treat their workers that way," Owen said.

"I wonder what the extent of it is," May mused.

Owen narrowed his eyes thoughtfully.

"Maybe they're employing more of these illegal workers than we thought? Maybe it's a bigger thing? Maybe they're totally illegal and they're being threatened or blackmailed, or somehow coerced into staying?"

May nodded.

"Given that staffing is their main cost, imagine if they could cut that right down? They'd be in a position to make a huge profit, even if the hotels weren't fully busy."

She thought back to what the article, and the business editor, had explained to her. Staffing was by far the biggest financial burden for a hotel.

"If there's more going on, how do we find out?" Owen asked.

"I think we need to go back there," May said.

"To where?" Owen asked.

"To the hotel where we met Mr. Reed. The Mount Amethyst is one of the places he owns. Let's go and speak to the maid we saw there and ask her what the Reeds are hiding. I want to know, from her, what her situation is and if there are any problems with it. And I also want to know why she seems so scared."

CHAPTER TWENTY ONE

May had thought her plan seemed like a brilliant idea when she was pacing up and down in the warm sunshine outside the police department, her mind racing at top speed.

Now that she and Owen were pulling up outside the Mount Amethyst, she felt nervous and doubtful all over again.

What if her theory was wrong?

Going up to this imposing hotel, she felt like an intruder, an unwanted and uninvited guest who was persisting in being a nuisance long after the case itself should be closed.

She knew she was only here because she was so sure that there was something else going on here at the hotel. Something that could be important to the case.

She was determined to find out what that something else was. If only she had access to the FBI databases. If only she could send agents in to do a raid for undocumented workers.

But she couldn't. May had none of that at her disposal. All she had were herself, Owen, and an idea that something was wrong. All she could do was arrive here, hoping that if she got face to face with the right people, she could find out the truth.

She turned to Owen, and he looked at her.

"Are you ready to do this?" he asked.

She nodded, and he nodded back at her and got out of the car.

They walked up to the imposing entrance of the hotel. She felt nervous, but she was filled with determination. The answers were waiting inside, and all she had to do was find them.

"I'm here to see Mr. Reed," she told the receptionist.

The woman looked surprised. "You're back?"

"Yes. We have a couple more questions."

"Please go over to the elevator."

There was the selfsame guard waiting by the doors. Thickset, muscular, and with a distinctly unfriendly demeanor.

"What do you want?" he asked.

"We need to go up to Mr. Reed's penthouse," May said.

The guard looked her up and down.

"Mr. Reed is not in. If he's not in, he doesn't allow visitors."

Owen stepped forward. "We're the police," he said politely, showing his badge.

The guard folded his arms.

"Where's your warrant?" he asked. "This is private property."

"We've been up before. We just need to do some further research," May countered.

"That was when Mr. Reed was here. He's not here now."

She was beginning to feel deeply suspicious about the amount of security that this hotel had in operation. This wasn't just to make sure Mr. Reed stayed safe. This was to keep inquiring people at bay. She felt sure of it.

"We're investigating a murder. We don't need a warrant to go up there," Owen explained.

The guard snorted.

"Mr. Reed does not want any more harassment from the police. You've already been here asking him questions. He does not want to be questioned by you again."

"That was a private interview," Owen replied. "We've got a new angle on the case we're investigating. We just want to talk to a few of the people who work for him."

May was glad he didn't specify which one. She had a strong feeling that if he had, that maid would have vanished from the premises.

Something was very wrong here, and now that they were digging in the right place, they were coming up against enough resistance to increase her suspicions.

The guard folded his arms and looked as if he wasn't going to budge.

"We're not leaving," May said firmly.

"We can't let you in, ma'am. If you want to go upstairs then I suggest you come back with the warrant."

"That's ridiculous," Owen said.

"It's not up to you. It's not up to me. I'm just telling you. Mr. Reed does not want any more police. He has nothing more to say. He does not want you talking to his staff. This is private property. And he feels the murders are linked to their personal life. Nothing to do with the business."

"I've got a right to investigate the case. I can't confirm what he thinks unless I am able to ask the questions I need to," May pressed him.

"I've got a job to do here," the guard replied. "And you're not seeing anyone." His voice suddenly took on a threatening tone.

May was feeling more and more uneasy.

This was a hotel run by ruthless, wealthy people. What was it they were trying to hide? Why were they being so unhelpful, so aggressive, so defensive?

May knew she was going to have to find another way to get the information she needed. Being upfront wasn't working. Being the police wasn't working either.

So therefore, she was going to have to be sneaky. And if that meant running a risk to her own safety, then that was what she was going to have to do.

She shrugged, then nodded at Owen.

"We're going now," she said.

"I'm glad to hear it," the guard replied.

"We're leaving, but we'll be back. And when we come back, we'll have a warrant."

The guard smiled triumphantly, as if he'd won.

He turned back to his post, and May followed Owen out of the hotel and back down the steps. Just before they got to the car, Owen turned to her.

"Do you think we'll be able to get a warrant?" he muttered. "The longer I stood there, the more convinced I became that there's something underhanded going on. But what proof do we have when they're making it so difficult for us to do our research?"

"I know," May said.

"So what are we going to do?" Owen sounded downcast. "How are we going to find out? Shall we ask Sheriff Jack if there's any possibility of obtaining a warrant? Or do you think we should consider an alternative idea?" he asked, sounding more hopeful.

"I think the alternative idea will be quicker," May said.

Owen's face lit up. May could see he was longing to stick it to the hotel after the rude treatment they'd received inside.

"What's the plan?" he asked. "While we were standing there, I thought we should sneak around the back and see if we can speak to anyone else."

"That's exactly what I thought too. Let's sneak around the back. We need to lurk around the service entrance until we can see how to get in without alerting security. There's bound to be a way. And then we have to find the maid ourselves and ask her the questions we need to," May said.

The look on Owen's face was a mix of delight and fear.

"Are you sure you want to do this?" he asked.

"No," May replied.

"Do you think it's too dangerous?"

"Yes," May said bluntly.

"So why do you want to do it?"

"Because I'm not going to give up on this until I have the answers I need," she told him. "Because I'm not going to be stopped by some goons with guns. We need to know what's going on in that hotel. We'll only be able to find something out if we're able to get in without anyone knowing."

CHAPTER TWENTY TWO

May felt filled with resolve as she and Owen prowled around the hotel. There had to be a service entrance, an unguarded way in. Or at any rate, a less guarded way in. That was what she was looking for. A side entrance she could sneak through. A back door that was open for deliveries.

She didn't want to get caught. She didn't want to get stopped. It might lead to terrible trouble. But she was desperate to get answers.

She wondered what Kerry would have done in her situation. She had no idea. She knew her sister probably wouldn't have ended up in this predicament because the FBI had more clout. Her sister would probably have been able to intimidate that guard into letting her through. Or maybe just charm him, depending on her mood.

But May hadn't and couldn't. This was all new territory. Confusing, unsettling, and a little bit terrifying.

She was determined to wade into the unknown and face whatever she had to. After all, there was nothing stopping her asking questions of employees.

Nothing except the mogul owner who had secrets to hide and had ordered her off site, and a security team that seemed to be larger than the entire complement of the Fairshore police department.

"There's a door on the side. I wonder where that goes," Owen said.

May took a look at it. It did seem to be a way in, around the corner, hidden from sight.

"Let's see if it's open," she said.

Even as she said it, she suddenly felt a shiver run down her back. She felt like there was someone watching her, about to shout at her or call a guard. She had to fight the urge to turn around and look guiltily behind her. The borderline between what they were and were not permitted to do was already blurred at best, exceeded at worst.

May told herself to keep her head straight, stay calm, and do the things she needed to do.

She pushed the door, and let out a deep sigh of relief when it opened wide.

"Hello?" she called softly, in case there was anyone nearby.

No reply.

"Hello?" she said again. "Is anyone there?"

Again, no reply.

Deciding that this gave her unspoken permission to go a little further, she stepped inside, and then she and Owen looked around.

They were in a service corridor. There was a cloakroom to their left, and a storeroom full of cleaning products on their right.

Ahead, the corridor branched. On their right, it seemed the passage led to the hotel kitchens. She could see brighter light ahead, and smell the delicious aroma of food.

On the left, was a door marked *"Private—No Entry."*

"What is this place?" Owen asked, looking at the door.

"I think it might lead to the staff area," May told him.

"Which way should we go?"

May considered.

"I don't want to go into the kitchens. It's not private enough. I think we go to the left, if it's not locked," she said. "Hopefully some of the staff are in their own rooms, or their lounge, or whatever's behind there."

She was feeling more and more uneasy. That door was dingy looking, dented and old. It didn't seem like it belonged in the hotel at all.

"Okay," Owen said. He sounded nervous.

"I have a weird feeling about this," May said.

"About what? This is the only way we're going to get any answers about what's going on with that building."

"I know. But it just feels like...like something is off-kilter here," she said.

"I know what you mean. But there's nobody around, so I guess we just push on."

"It's kind of creepy," she said. She had a cold feeling that she was making more than just a choice about which way to go, that if they went through the door, they would be escalating their risk.

But May told herself to get a grip.

They had already made a deal to sneak around the hotel. To get into places they didn't belong. To try to confirm her strong suspicion that something here was deeply wrong and the hotel was doing whatever they could to cover it up. This was just the next step.

They pushed open the access door and May walked into a narrow passage. It smelled damp and dusty. It was semi dark. And it was lined with doors.

"Are these the staff's bedrooms?" Owen whispered.

"I guess they must be," May said.

May knocked on one, her stomach churning. There was no answer.

Moving along, she knocked on the next.

A woman's voice called out a question in a language they didn't understand.

"Sorry," May said. "Sorry, we don't understand you. Do you speak English?"

There was silence.

Then the door opened.

May found herself staring into the face of someone who could have been the maid's sister. She was tall, slim, blonde, in her twenties, and she looked terrified.

Beyond her, the small room contained a double bed with a white coverlet, a small wardrobe, and a bathroom cubicle. It was like the most basic, spartan motel room May had ever seen.

There were no photos in the room. No paintings. There were no books. No little things. No signs of personality. Just a room that someone had moved into.

No window, just a ventilation grille and a fan.

"We're police," May said. "Do you work for the hotel?"

The woman stared back at her and May saw even more terror in her eyes.

With a terrible sinking feeling in her stomach, she was starting to understand what really must be going on here.

"You speak English, don't you?" May insisted. "Please, talk to us."

But again, the woman said nothing. She just stared at them.

"Please, I only work here. I do not know anything," she whispered eventually.

"We're not going to cause any trouble," May said. "We just want to ask you some questions."

"No police. Never police. I don't know anything. Please, go away," the woman said. Her words were fast, panicked.

It was clear that the maid was petrified to be caught talking to them.

May and Owen stepped inside the room. Then May turned around and closed the door. She knew this was their only chance.

"We are investigating a crime," she whispered. "I promise you, you are not in trouble and this is not a trap. If we get the right information, things could change for you. If we leave, things might never change. What do you want?"

May stared at her, letting her decide for herself.

"Okay," the maid whispered.

"What's your name?" May then asked.

"Anya."

"Please tell me. What goes on here?" May asked calmly. "We need to know. We want to try and help the people. We have a feeling things are not right here."

The woman looked at her for a moment, her face sheet white.

"No," she admitted in a low voice. "Nothing is right."

"You can tell us," May said. She kept her voice low, her manner soothing.

"I can tell you. But you must not tell anyone else, or I will get into trouble."

"Why?"

Anya looked around, as if she were checking to see that nobody was listening.

"I have a passport, no visa. But I cannot go home because they took my passport when I arrived here. I must work. I am here on a contract. When I finish my contract, I will receive my green card. But the contract is not like they said it would be. We have to work without pay for a long time. All we receive is a room and basic items and our food."

"How long?" May asked, feeling a terrible coldness inside. This was horrific.

"Ten years," the woman said sadly and Owen gasped.

This was slavery, pure and simple.

The puzzle pieces were falling into place for May.

Now she was starting to understand why Madeline had made so many trips to Eastern Europe. She wasn't just bringing back temporary workers on the cheap. She was not looking to bypass visa requirements. She was bringing in slaves, who would be imprisoned, helpless and terrified, to work at no cost in Reed Leisure hotels. And perhaps other places, too. May wondered whether this might just be the start, the tip of an iceberg.

"How many workers are there here?" May asked.

"Twenty of us, between this hotel and one other," Anya replied.

"Have you been in this hotel long?" May asked.

"Almost a year," the woman said.

"How did you come here?"

"I was waitressing in Slovakia. And this woman called Madeline came to my restaurant. She seemed really nice. She told me there were opportunities in the hospitality industry in the USA, that I could be working there instead and earning ten times as much. That I could have a life there. I believed her. She organized me a flight and a visa. But only a vacation visa," she said sadly. "She said the real one would be arranged on arrival. But when I got here, everything was different. They said that I owed them a lot of money and that I would need to work to pay it off. But every time we make mistakes, the time gets longer."

May nodded sadly. She could just imagine how this woman's spirit had been broken.

"I don't go outside, except to go to work. We are not allowed to leave the grounds at all. We know if we are found, we will be punished. Our time working for the hotel will be longer. Or else, worse things. We could be imprisoned. We will have a criminal record and spend many years here locked away. Or the guards will deal with us, and that is the worst of all."

May glanced at Owen. He was looking back at her with a grim expression, as if he was thinking the same thing she was.

They had to get them out of there. They had to get help for this woman and the others like her who were trapped in this hotel.

But May wanted to find out more. She was sure there was more to learn.

She took a deep breath, ready to ask the next question, the one that she hoped would add the final pieces to the puzzle.

And then, from the other side of the door they'd entered, came the tramp of heavy footsteps, approaching purposefully.

May's heart was banging in her chest. She didn't want to imagine what would happen if the wrong person walked into this room now.

Anya put a terrified finger over her lips. They all froze in place.

May crossed her fingers, feeling cold inside about what the consequences might be.

CHAPTER TWENTY THREE

"Be quiet," Anya breathed to May. She looked about to burst into tears as the footsteps came closer.

May watched the door, feeling as if she'd gotten herself embroiled into a nightmare that had exploded out of all proportions.

And then, the footsteps passed by. She heard the squeak of hinges as a door ahead opened, and the sound of low voices. Then the door closed.

"That is one of the guards," the woman explained. Her eyes were brimming with tears. "They come here sometimes. Some of us—we are willing to do extra things, in exchange for money, so we can pay off our debt to the hotel sooner."

"That's terrible," Owen breathed. He looked utterly appalled.

"The women who choose to do this usually get paid five dollars a time," Anya explained. "I do not choose to do this. But for some, they hope they can get out faster this way. It is better than living like this. Better than staying here, in this prison."

May glanced at Owen.

The five-dollar bill stuffed into the throats of the two victims was no coincidence. This was all leading back to the same set of circumstances.

May simply couldn't believe that such a dreadful, abusive practice was taking place—in their own county! These women, who were being held against their will and forced into slavery and prostitution, were living just a few miles from their own town.

She knew that there was a problem with human trafficking in the US, and it was constantly on the news. But to her, it had always seemed to be something that happened in other places. Not right on her own doorstep. In her jurisdiction.

"Please, can you give me some more information?" she said. "Who are the people who are abusing you, who are sleeping with you?"

The woman's eyes filled with tears.

"You promise me you will help us?" she asked. "Please, you must help us."

May looked at Owen, who nodded.

"I promise you," May said. She wasn't going to leave until she had a plan of action in place.

But first, she needed as many facts as she could get. There were now two crimes they had to deal with. Human trafficking and murder. Undoubtedly they were related to the same set of activities.

"How many hotels are involved? Is it just here in Minnesota? Do you know?"

Anya tilted her head. "The guards, they sometimes talk."

That was lucky, May thought.

"What do they say?"

"I think there are only two hotels involved so far. This one, which is the Mount Amethyst, and another one, which is the Lakeside Heights. I have never been there. But from what the guards overhear and tell us, they are planning more. I believe it is very successful. They are making a lot of money without paying for any cleaning or waitressing services. The hotels have become extremely profitable. The guards said they are going to recruit builders next. Then models, to be used in a few of the strip clubs that this company owns." Her voice was bitter.

May had a feeling that Reed Leisure had long-term plans, and that Madeline's death would be only a temporary spoke in the wheel. She was sure that having seen how lucrative this model was, Bert Reed would want to use it over and over.

Slavery was the cheapest form of labor.

They wouldn't have to pay a salary. They wouldn't have to pay for cleaning or waitressing services, or even for the labor costs in the hotel's new wing. All they would have to do was source the workers.

It was a sickening thought.

"So only the two hotels?" May's mind was already racing. "Anya, please tell me. This is very important. Who are the men who sleep with you?"

"One of them was Danny. The hotel builder, or the architect, I think. He sleeps with whoever he can. He is a monster, and abusive. Then there are some of the guards who do the same, and also a few of the other managers and workers. The manager, Lewis, is one of the worst. He was very close to the woman who brought us here. He was, like, her second in command, and seems to know everything. He was the one who took our passports and kept them. He punishes us if we get out of line, and he takes videos of what he does."

"We've heard of Lewis. Can you tell me all the other names you know?" Owen asked softly. "Or better still, write them down for me?"

"Sure. I do not know them all, but I know some names."

Anya took the pen and began writing.

As she did, May thought about what she'd said. Danny was dead.

Was the killer punishing everyone involved in this scheme? May thought so. In that case, Lewis might well be targeted next, as Madeline's second in command who had most likely taken over when she started to realize the FBI was scrutinizing her.

But how was she going to find the killer? And where would this killer strike again?

"Has anyone tried to escape?" she asked, wondering if anyone had.

Anya nodded.

"Two girls tried. One, Katia, was punished so badly I could not tell you what she went through. She was moved to the other hotel. And the other, Zinaida, disappeared. They said that they found her body, but never told us how she died." Anya paused. "Another woman, Laima, died here before I arrived. She was sleeping with men to try and pay her way out faster. Something went wrong, and she was killed."

"Has anyone ever tried to help you?" Surely someone could have done something, May wondered.

Anya nodded again. "Last year, one of the hotel's waiters found out and became very angry. But he was instantly fired. I don't think he had the chance to try and help us, but we still hope."

"What was his name?"

"His name was Sam. I don't know his last name."

A waiter called Sam. Was he the killer? Had Sam come back to try and get revenge on these atrocities?

May was sure the Reeds must have threatened Sam in every way possible with their powerful team of lawyers. Perhaps he'd been coerced in other ways, too. Who knew how far they would have gone to protect their interests?

They were all quiet again as more footsteps tramped into what May now thought of as the slaves' quarters.

May knew they were going to run out of time if they stayed here. There was going to be more and more risk of being discovered.

She turned to Owen. He was staring back at her, his eyes full of concern and intensity.

"Thank you," she said, and squeezed the woman's hand. She wanted to tell her she wasn't alone, that they would make sure that she was rescued, but she didn't dare.

She didn't want to give this woman or any of the others hope before she was sure they were out of danger here.

Anya did not say anything. Her face was stained with tears, and her eyes were wide with terror. She did not look like she believed anything would ever change.

But May was committed to doing just that.

She was going to find the killer and save the women. She just needed an urgent plan, and to figure out where to start.

"Thank you," May said. "Thank you so much for talking to us. I know it must have been hard."

The woman nodded. May and Owen went to the door, and after they stepped out, the woman closed it. May heard a key turn in the lock.

The two of them silently returned to the back corridor and then made their way to the side entrance. Tiptoeing along, all May was thinking of doing was getting out as quickly and quietly as she could. But her mind was running a hundred miles an hour.

"We can't leave this," she muttered. "We have to get help for the girls immediately. But at the same time, we have to find this killer."

Suddenly, the task confronting her seemed enormous, insurmountable. She needed to get Sheriff Jack involved. The entire resources of Tamarack County's police department would be needed to make sure this operation was a success. There were so many people involved.

But even so, May knew that the personnel manager, Lewis Brooks, was a key witness who knew a lot of information. He held the passports. He had video footage. His knowledge would be important now that Madeline had died. These people seemed to operate in secrecy and silos. If one died, it was a circuit breaker. That was how they thought. Danny had proved it.

And, given how closely he was involved in these misdoings, the killer would undoubtedly be targeting Lewis next. That meant their primary source of evidence was at risk.

If Lewis died, it might even mean the case fell apart.

May knew she had to find him immediately, before the killer did.

CHAPTER TWENTY FOUR

"We have to rescue these women as soon as we can," May told Owen in a low voice, as they walked back to the car, trying to look like they were strolling around the hotel. It felt almost impossible to walk casually while under such pressure.

If anyone saw them now, it would mean such deep trouble! May knew they didn't have time. These women were nothing more than disposable assets to the hotel. Who knew what might happen to them if Reed and his security team found out that May and Owen had learned the truth? They might be moved, hidden away, or worse.

She and Owen couldn't let that happen.

Owen nodded. "I agree. But we need to get a team involved. So many women, being held at two hotels?"

May nodded. "Yes. We're going to need a lot of resources on it in a very short time. But in the meantime, the killer is on the loose. And there's a big possibility that he—or she—is going to target the person who's the next most complicit in this entire trafficking ring, and who holds all the important info that will make or break the case."

"Lewis Brooks," Owen agreed.

"So we need to make this a two-pronged operation. The first prong is to rescue these girls, raid the hotels, and hold all the guards and management in custody until we know who is guilty."

"And the second prong is to find the killer," Owen said.

"Exactly."

They needed help. What they needed was manpower, and a plan that could save the women. The stakes were high, the danger was real, and the clock was ticking.

She reached the car and they got in. Closing the door, she breathed a quiet sigh of relief that they'd made it this far. Meanwhile, her thoughts were accelerating.

They needed to make sure that this trafficking operation was shut down once and for all, and that all the people involved were punished to the full extent of the law.

But at the same time, they had to stop the killer and prevent the next kingpin in this ugly game from falling prey to murder.

A plan was beginning to form in May's mind. She saw what the outline of it would be.

"I'm going to call Jack right now," she said.

Squaring her shoulders, she voiced what she had realized in the past few minutes that she needed to accept.

"It's an international trafficking case, and we're going to need a massive amount of resources. I'm pretty sure Jack will immediately request that we get the FBI involved in the trafficking side."

May felt surprised by her own thoughts. Initially she'd been jealous and protective over this case, fearful that her sister would muscle in and take it away from her. But now she saw how helpful the FBI could be, and how badly they needed every agent that they could get in order to capture the trafficking ring and save the imprisoned women. As the deputy, it was the right decision for her to call in the FBI immediately, and one that her superiors would approve of.

It felt liberating that she could perceive things this way.

Feeling positive, May picked up the phone.

She needed to tell Jack everything, and fast, to get the raid under way. She needed to make sure that Lewis didn't end up dead. And she needed to figure out how to dovetail the two priorities.

"Please let this go smoothly," she said under her breath.

She dialed the number. She could feel Owen's eyes on her. The phone rang. Once, twice, three times. Then Jack answered.

"May. What's happening. Any update?"

May took a deep breath.

"Jack, this is much bigger than we thought. Much more complex. The people who have been targeted by the killer are involved in a trafficking ring, bringing slave labor to two Reed Leisure hotels in the area."

There was a pause at the other end.

"What?" Jack said. He sounded incredulous.

"The women are from Eastern Europe," May said. "They are all brought in on tourist visas and they are staying at the Mount Amethyst and the Lakeside Heights. There are plans to bring in more and expand, but for now I think they're in those locations only."

"Go on?" Jack said.

"They're treated very badly and made to work hard labor for no pay. There's also prostitution involved. I believe there are plans to bring in more workers, and those will be channeled to the strip clubs and the building of the new wing. Madeline was the main person spearheading this project but she was assisted by Lewis Brooks, who's the hotel's personnel manager. I think she handed the reins to him when she realized the FBI was paying her attention. He now has all the details on the women and holds their passports as well as video footage."

"Right. Got you. Go on," Jack said.

"Lewis Brooks will have a massive amount of information, as he's deeply involved, but the problem is that the killer seems to be targeting everyone at the top of this operation."

"So you're concerned Lewis might be killed before he can be questioned regarding the trafficking?"

"Yes, I am," May said.

"That's a definite concern. This is far bigger than we thought. We need to act on it as fast as possible," Jack said.

"Jack, this is deep and widespread. This requires manpower and a lot of resources. I think we need to involve the FBI, and we need to assemble a team and raid the two hotels and make arrests," May said.

She was surprised to realize that as she said it, she meant every word.

Jack said, "I'm going to contact the other police in Tamarack County, May. I'll call the FBI directly and let them know we need their help immediately."

"My sister Kerry's in town. She was the agent that handled the serial case last time. I'm sure she could respond quickly, and get a team of agents to work with the police."

"That's good to know and will make things go even faster," Jack said.

May felt reluctant, as if she were handing over everything she'd worked toward, again. But then Jack continued.

"The murder is a separate issue, and it's even more urgent. So while I am organizing the raids, I need you to bring in Lewis Brooks, as I agree he is likely to be the next target based on the killer's pattern. Let's get him into police custody where the killer can't target him. We need to bring him in using a way that won't arouse suspicion or cause any risk to the women. And once he's inside, you need to focus on finding the killer."

"That sounds perfect, Jack," May said, relieved that she still had control over the core part of her case.

"I'll be coordinating with the FBI and the other police departments in Tamarack County, and getting other people involved in the trafficking raid. I'm calling them now, and I want to be updated on any developments as soon as you have them."

"Will do," May said.

And May, I trust your instincts," Jack said. "I know you know what you're doing, and I know you can handle this. But you also need to be careful. The killer is likely to be active right now, and you and Owen might be in danger."

CHAPTER TWENTY FIVE

May knew her first priority was to locate Lewis Brooks. But she needed to do it in a way that would keep her under the hotel's radar. She couldn't afford to warn Lewis, or he would undoubtedly flee and destroy all the precious evidence he held. She couldn't afford to raise suspicions any higher, or it would mean a massive danger for the trafficked women.

"They're alerted to us at the Mount Amethyst," she told Owen. "We can't go back there again or they're going to know something's afoot. So, perhaps our best bet is to speak to Jolene at the Lakeside Heights. She doesn't know that we've been to the Mount Amethyst. I'm sure they haven't gotten around to telling her yet."

"That's a great idea," Owen said.

"I don't know where Lewis could be. If he works for the group, he could be anywhere. But as the manager, she might know his schedule, or be able to find out for us."

May knew there was only one way she was going to be able to prevent Jolene from warning Lewis, and that was to take her into custody. So they would have to persuade her that this was being done for her own safety and that she, too, was in danger. Well, for all May knew, she was. She had no idea how long the killer's hit list was, or who else might be on it.

They drove away from the Mount Amethyst. As the road scrolled by, May went through her plans in her mind.

Firstly, get Jolene into custody so she couldn't warn Lewis, or anyone else. Secondly, find Lewis's whereabouts, hopefully before the killer got to him. And thirdly, arrest him—and with any luck, locate the killer, too.

It was a lot to do.

"I think we should go in two separate cars," Owen said. " Then one of us can take Jolene in, and the other can go straight on to wherever she says Lewis is."

"That's a great idea," May said. "Let's go back via the police department, so we're both mobile. It's on the way and will only take a minute, and then we won't waste any time on the hunt."

Fifteen minutes later, May screeched to a stop outside the Lakeside Heights Hotel. Owen scrambled out of his car behind her, and they headed up to the hotel. May felt breathless and resolute. She walked into reception, knowing that she had to appear confident and not give anything away.

Even so, out of the corner of her eye, she saw a uniformed cleaner walking quickly down the corridor, her head bowed, and May's instincts were instantly sparked. Was this one of the trafficked slaves at work? Now, she suspected strongly it was. But she couldn't give her suspicions away.

She dragged her focus back to the receptionist's stare.

"Is your manager available?" she asked, showing her badge. "We have some important information on the recent murders."

"Sure."

A moment later, with a click of heels, Jolene breezed in.

"Good afternoon, Deputies. Is there any news?" she asked.

Was it May's imagination or did she also look briefly in the cleaner's direction?

"Good afternoon, ma'am. We've had a breakthrough in the case. We understand that the killer is planning on targeting key people in the hotel's management. It's someone with a grudge against the business. We're still working on the details," May explained, playing on what she knew Jolene already believed.

"Is that so?" Now, Jolene looked alarmed.

"There's a possibility that you may be targeted, Ms. Barr. For your own safety we would like you to come into the police department for the next few hours, until we can hunt the killer down."

"But I—are you sure?"

Fear for her own safety was overriding Jolene's suspicions about their sudden appearance here. May knew, from watching her face, that she was likely to agree.

"It's very important, ma'am. As you are aware, this killer can strike at any time, and has killed near this hotel before. If you stay here, you'll be at serious risk. Your presence might also endanger your fellow workers."

"Oh, that's terrible. That's really scary. I can't put anyone else at risk. Alright, I'll come with you."

Grabbing her purse from the desk, Jolene walked out with May and Owen.

Now that she was out of the hotel environment, May needed to ask the important question that would hopefully lead them to the killer. As they hustled to the parking lot, she spoke again.

"We're also looking to bring your personnel manager, Lewis Brooks, into a place of safety as he may be targeted as well. Do you know what his schedule is, and where he would be at this time of the day?"

"At this time?" She checked her watch and frowned. Looking at her, May could see she was in a state of anxiety and struggling to gather her thoughts. Then, sounding relieved, Jolene spoke. "He'll be at the hotel's main liquor warehouse. He goes there twice a week to pay the casual staff and check their hours."

"And where is that?"

"In the industrial estate on the outskirts of Misty Hills. It's at Four Appletree Road."

May nodded. She knew where that was.

The clock was ticking, but now they had a strong lead to their suspect. Jolene climbed into the back of the cruiser and Owen sped away. Watching them go, May felt a huge sense of relief that Jolene hadn't been able to warn her boss, or tell him what the police had asked.

They were only just in time. As May was about to get inside her car and head off to the warehouse, she saw a big black Range Rover accelerating into the hotel.

The car roared up the drive, barely swerving to avoid Owen's departing cruiser, and pulled up right in front of the entrance with a screech of brakes.

May stood up straighter as the driver's door opened and a security guard climbed out.

He walked around to the other side of the car and opened the door for none other than Bert Reed. The beautiful assistant scrambled out of the back on her own.

Finally, May was realizing why he surrounded himself with this level of security. There was a good reason for it. He knew he could be a target.

The hotel mogul glowered at May.

"I heard you were interfering earlier. My staff sent you away from the Mount Amethyst and told you to obtain a warrant. Now you're here? What's going on? Do you have a warrant? If not, I must demand that you leave our premises. You are on private property without permission. I have a series of meetings now that can't be interrupted."

May felt filled with relief that this unpleasant man had not arrived five minutes earlier. If he had, they would never have been able to ask Jolene what they needed to, or take her away.

As it was, his manager was on her way to the police department, where May was sure Owen would insist that she hand in her phone immediately.

"Just following up," May said innocently. "We're on the trail of the murder suspect and hope to make an arrest very soon."

She didn't add that the arrest would hopefully be Bert Reed himself, when the place was raided. At least his meetings meant he'd be on site when the FBI arrived, which would be good.

Bert's glower faded slightly. The security guard was still staring at her mistrustfully, with his arms folded. The personal assistant was rummaging in her purse, looking for something.

"You are that close to finding them? Well, that's good. That'll be good. Yes." Then Bert's face darkened again. "You know, it's more likely to be something to do with Madeline's and Danny's personal lives. You do know that, right? We run a clean business here. There's no need to pry into our affairs."

"We're just doing our job, sir," May replied, keeping her voice calm and level, in spite of her rising fury at his attempt to intimidate her.

"I'm doing the same," came the snide comeback. "I run this hotel, something that you do not. I have a right to ensure it runs smoothly. I don't trust one bit that the police department is not as prejudiced as the locals are."

"I understand that, sir," May confirmed, biting her tongue and wishing she could say more.

It was satisfying to think that right now, Kerry was swinging into action and that the full might of the FBI would be coming down on the hotel and hopefully saving these terrified and abused women from their plight.

Who would have thought, a day ago, that she'd actually appreciate her sister helping with a case and be grateful for her actions?

But in the meantime, May couldn't delay.

Lewis Brooks was still a target and if he was killed, the evidence trail and the plans would be much harder to track.

Her priority now was to race to the warehouse and get to Lewis before the killer found him.

CHAPTER TWENTY SIX

May climbed in her cruiser and sped away from the hotel's premises. It was now after five-thirty p.m. and she hoped Lewis would still be at the warehouse. And that he was still alive.

She raced through town, then turned left onto the main road out of town that would take her to Misty Hills.

The killer had to be Sam, the ex-employee, May decided. Sam would have known the ins and outs of the hotel. And the killings had been very carefully planned and stealthily done.

May knew that getting to the warehouse as soon as possible was crucial. She didn't want to take any chances that Bert Reed might put two and two together and decide to warn Lewis, after finding that Jolene was no longer at the hotel. She wanted to get there before Bert had the chance to make any calls.

She pushed her foot down hard on the accelerator and flew along the road, weaving around the slower vehicles. As she sped on, she wondered what she would find when she reached the warehouse. May knew she needed to be prepared for any eventuality.

There was the industrial estate up ahead. The industrial area of Misty Hills was very small, just a couple of blocks in size, and Appletree Road was a short one, with only five neat warehouses along it.

She turned into the street and wove through the warehouse lots until she spotted the one she was looking for.

She had no time to waste.

There it was. Number four.

Was he here? There were a few cars parked nearby, but the parking area looked to be shared. She couldn't tell if he was here. It was time to go inside and see what she could find.

May walked up to the warehouse. The door was closed. But when she pushed it, it swung open.

So someone was inside. She felt extremely nervous as she stepped in.

The place smelled musty, with a hint of alcohol infusing the air. It was a spacious warehouse, with rows and rows of boxes and barrels and stacks of cans lining the tall steel shelves.

"Hello? Lewis Brooks?" she called out.

May waited. No answer.

Was anyone here? Did something happen?

She paced through the warehouse, feeling more and more jumpy with every step she took. She had the feeling something had gone wrong. Why was nobody around? Where was Lewis? Had Jolene lied to them or deliberately sent them in the wrong direction?

Her heart sped up as she worried that her side, a critical part of the operation's success, would prove to be the weak point that brought the whole operation down.

What if she was to fail while her sister succeeded? May couldn't bear the thought of that happening. Now she was beginning to think her decision to involve the FBI hadn't been so intelligent after all.

And yet, what option did they have? Rescuing the trafficked women was the priority and that was firmly under the FBI's jurisdiction. Even if she had ended up pursuing the more difficult and elusive lead as a result.

What if he was here, but already dead?

A shiver went through May at that thought. She began peering more closely into the aisles, looking for any sign that a body might have been abandoned.

Those big beer vats would be the ideal dumping ground for a body, especially since this killer seemed to use any container he or she could find for the step of drowning. The idea made chills rush through her but she knew she had to explore it.

May walked to the row of beer vats, checking each one carefully.

She jumped as she heard a clang behind her, and spun around.

But it must have been a bird landing on the steel roof, because the warehouse was empty and silent.

She carefully checked the rest of the warehouse. She walked past the beer vats and the row of barrels and cans. She looked at all the tall shelves, filled with boxes and crates. She even looked behind the motorized racking.

Nothing.

She was getting more and more worried that she was too late, and that something had gone wrong.

Maybe Jolene had made a mistake. Perhaps Lewis wasn't really here. Maybe he'd changed his schedule. Or maybe he was dead.

May shook her head, trying to stop herself from spiraling down that particular path. She couldn't afford to worry about that possibility.

There was no sign of a fight or a struggle at all. Not in here. But there was also no sign of Lewis.

"Lewis Brooks?" she called again. But there was no reply. She'd now reached the other end of the warehouse, with no sign of his presence at all.

He must have gone somewhere else, or been forcibly taken. And she had no idea where that might be.

There was nothing else to do. If she was going to track him down, she was going to have to call Owen and ask him to ask Jolene if she had any other ideas where this man might be.

Standing uneasily in the empty warehouse, she dialed Owen's number, hoping he'd pick up. Time was ticking by. She felt desperate that she was going to mess up her part in this vital operation.

Please answer, she worried, as she listened to the phone ring.

Then Owen grabbed it, sounding breathless. "May! What's happening? Have you found him?"

She could hear the panic in her own voice as she updated him.

"He's not here! I have no idea where he is! Owen, is there any way you might be able to ask Jolene for other ideas? How's it going that side?"

"Well, everything here is going at full speed," Owen said. "Your sister has arrived, and a team from the FBI Minneapolis office is about ten minutes away. She's organizing things as we speak so that there are no delays. The raids are all on track. They'll be setting off any minute. I'm joining the team to raid the Mount Amethyst as we're still two officers short."

"That's all sounding good," May said, feeling sick inside.

It was just her letting the team down. Just her! It wasn't her fault, but she had to fix it.

"Jolene is in one of the interview rooms. She's given me some very interesting information. She says she's been here two months and is very worried about some of the things they've been doing. She actually told me she sent an anonymous tip-off to Emily, asking her to investigate the hotel, because she thought there was underhanded business going on. But every time she asks questions, she's threatened with being fired and being sued. So she's kept quiet until now."

"That's interesting," May said. Now the pieces were starting to fit together. It also meant Jolene was honest, and would try to give them reliable information.

"I've taken her phone away. She'll remain in the police station for the duration of the evening and she's happy to give evidence. I'll go in again and ask her about this."

May waited, shifting from foot to foot. How could this be happening? How could she be the weakest link?

Perhaps Jolene would know. May held her breath as she waited for Owen's reply.

He came back sounding disappointed.

"Unfortunately she says she has no idea. He always went there and would usually return to the hotel at about six-thirty p.m. I don't know what else to suggest, May. Maybe they'll pick up Lewis in one of the raids."

May thought frantically. If Lewis had suddenly disappeared, then it meant he was already on the run. But maybe he was still somewhere in the area, especially if this was his confirmed location.

"Did Jolene ever go to the warehouse herself?" She wanted to know if the manager had a picture of the warehouse in her mind.

After a pause, Owen replied.

"She says no."

So she had no idea of the location or the layout. All she had was an address at which the stock was stored.

With May's brain now steaming, as she stared in despair at the scattering of vehicles outside, she came up with another question.

"What car does Lewis drive?"

Another pause.

"It's a red Honda hatchback. She doesn't know more than that."

"Okay. Thanks."

May had spied a red Honda among the parked cars. So his vehicle was here. She felt a sense of relief that at least he hadn't left. Had he been taken? she wondered with a chill. Had someone grabbed him and run?

But then another idea occurred to her.

Perhaps there was more than one warehouse belonging to the hotel in this row. After all, the warehouse was unlocked. That should have told her something. Nobody had locked up and gone home, and that might be because they were still here.

Perhaps there was another warehouse that housed the delivery trucks. They had to be somewhere, didn't they?

Eager to explore her theory, May walked out of the warehouse and turned to the right.

She saw a paved path leading to the next warehouse, and an open door beyond. That gave her a flare of hope.

Was this it? Was this where Lewis had gone?

May went to the door and tiptoed into the warehouse. Immediately, she gasped.

From at the back, she could hear shouts and screams, bangs and crashes. Something was happening. There was a big fight, a struggle ensuing.

Knowing now that she must absolutely be on the right track, May rushed inside.

CHAPTER TWENTY SEVEN

Inside the second warehouse was chaos. Instantly, the shouts and clangs grew louder. Glass was smashed on the floor and the sharp reek of spirits cut the air. Boxes lay on their sides. Barrels were upended. Cans were everywhere.

She had entered between two rows of shelves. But the main part of the warehouse was huge and this was where the bulk of the noise seemed to be coming from.

May rushed through. The noise definitely seemed to be coming from the back. It sounded like there was a fight going on.

One of the shelves had totally collapsed. Boxes were strewn in her path. As she carefully stepped over the spilled alcohol, May wondered what was happening.

She hurried forward, following the loud yelling she could hear.

The floor in this area was a pool of wine. Fragments of glass slipped and crunched under her boots. May drew her gun as she walked. She did not want to be overpowered by the killer, who she was certain must be here.

But, even though she could hear shouting, she couldn't see anyone, she realized. Where was the noise and banging coming from?

In front of her, a row of shelves had been pulled down, leading to the collapse of the other shelving. A couple were jammed together, blocking the path.

Quickly, she detoured around, seeing that she was almost at the end of the shelves. Beyond was a row of neatly parked trucks.

The banging and crashing were coming from the truck in the center. With her heart pounding in time with the metallic thumps, May tiptoed forward. It wasn't a fight, she realized. She'd been wrong about what she'd heard. Instead, someone was locked in the back. A man, from the shouts and screams.

"Help! Help me!" he was yelling.

May looked around cautiously. She couldn't see anyone else around. She paced toward the truck, making sure to watch her back.

"Who's there?" she called in a low voice, tapping on the van's steel back door.

There was silence.

Then a breathless, terrified voice answered.

"Lewis. I'm Lewis Brooks. And I fled here when some demented murderer tried to kill me in my office. Some crazed person wearing a big Joker mask attacked me."

"Is that so?"

May looked around, her hands feeling cold. Where was this Joker killer now?

From inside the truck, Lewis continued. "I was hit over the head. I almost passed out, but I managed to run. Then this person chased me. We ran through the warehouse and things got completely out of hand. They cut off my escape route so I took cover in here. I've locked myself in but I can't get out. It only opens from the outside. And I dropped my phone somewhere. I have no idea where it is!" He paused. "Who are you, anyway?"

"I'm going to get you out!" she explained, as she heard the heavy thudding of boots against the door. She had so much to do! She desperately needed to get this key witness into custody. And then she would have to rush straight back here and resume her hunt for the killer.

She tried the handle, but it didn't open.

Looking more closely, May saw it would need a key to be unlocked. That meant she now had to find the key, urgently.

"You're a brave woman. A very brave woman," Lewis replied.

May wasn't going to answer that. Not right now. Not when Lewis was headed straight for jail.

Despite the dangers that still loomed, her key witness was at least inside the truck. May felt a thread of relief that she had him at last. Let the FBI and other officers do their part in the raids and arrests. But she didn't need to wait for that. She had found her man.

For now, though, May had to figure out how to get him out. Once she had the key in her possession, she could unlock the back of the truck, draw her gun, make the arrest, and handcuff him. She could then march him to her vehicle, lock him in the back with his handcuffs secured, and she knew that she would be able to get him to the police department without any risk of having him escape along the way.

But finding the keys was a critical part of the operation.

She stepped away from the truck and looked around. Where would they be?

May took another look around, this time feeling panicked. She knew she had to work fast, because she had no idea where the killer had gone. With Lewis locked away and making such a terrible noise there was a chance that the killer had panicked and fled, but May acknowledged that this killer seemed to be an ice-cool operator. He or she had probably gone to look for more equipment to use against Lewis, seeing he had put up such a fight.

Or maybe the killer was looking for the keys, just like she was.

There were two large warehouses to be searched and limited time left to do it in.

Would the keys be kept in an office? Was there such a thing here?

May looked around. She didn't see anything nearby. No convenient shelf or ring or room where they could be stored. She walked toward the wall of the main warehouse, at one side of the rows of cars and trucks. If the keys were kept anywhere, surely it would be nearby?

There was a small office and when she looked inside, she saw no keys, only a laptop open on the desk. That must be where Lewis had been working. May felt sure they would need that laptop. It might be a treasure trove of information. She unplugged it and took it out to her car, checking around her carefully before locking it away in her trunk.

There was still nobody around. Was anyone watching her? Feeling spooked, May returned to the warehouse and continued looking for the keys.

In front of her, the shelving was stacked with boxes. To the left, she saw an open area with a couple of loose crates, but not much else. May decided to look in the crates.

As she reached them, she heard a noise from behind her. She spun around, looking into the shadows made by the high, stacked shelves. Her heart was hammering.

Nothing there.

And no sign of any office or key storage.

"Help me!" Lewis began yelling again. "Where have you gone?"

May looked around, feeling frantic. If her plan wouldn't work, then the only other solution would be to call for help and get someone in here to force the truck open. She really didn't want to do that as it would waste a lot of time and there was a killer on the loose, but there seemed to be no choice.

Then a last-minute idea occurred to her. Perhaps in this warehouse, which was locked overnight, it could be that the keys were in an obvious place.

She went back to the truck. It was the only place she hadn't looked.

May tried the driver's door. It opened smoothly.

Her first glance was at the ignition. That was where she'd hoped the keys would be but they weren't there. The ignition slot was empty.

The truck's cab was clean and neat. The leather seat looked pristine. There was a clipboard on the driver's seat which was presumably for deliveries.

May picked the keyboard up. And as she did so, she heard a jingle of metal and her heart leaped.

There were the keys. Neatly stowed in a clear plastic bag under the clipboard.

She had the keys. Now all she needed to do was open the truck, arrest her suspect, and get him back to the police department.

This was going to work out perfectly and May felt a surge of hope. She picked up the keys and started to turn. And then, her adrenaline spiked, as behind her, she sensed a figure looming.

May had the barest glimpse of a Joker's mask, its mouth set in a horrible, blood-red grin.

"No!" But she never had time to utter the word that flared in her mind.

Metal flashed as the figure lifted something high in the air. And then it crashed down on May's head, and the world sputtered into darkness.

CHAPTER TWENTY EIGHT

May was being tossed around, lashed from side to side, with an engine roaring in the background.

She tried to reach out a hand to save herself but she couldn't. She felt sick and dizzy and completely disoriented.

She opened her eyes. Her head was throbbing. Where was she? What was happening?

To her utter confusion, she found she was half-sprawled in the passenger seat of a truck. Her hands were tied behind her back with nylon rope. The truck's seatbelt was the only thing preventing her from going through the windshield or onto the floor in this crazy, rocketing drive.

May glanced to her left and, to her horror, saw the killer gripping the wheel.

The Joker mask looked garish and cruel in the dim, evening light. The truck's headlights cut the gathering gloom as they rushed along on a speedy, swaying ride that May feared was not going to end well.

From the back of the truck, she heard bangs and screams. Lewis was still locked inside. But the noise he was making wouldn't help, because the truck was flying along the back roads, taking quiet routes, jolting over rutted, seldom-used tracks.

May managed to get her legs working and wedged herself into a more stable position.

What should she do?

She guessed she could find out if the killer really was Sam. She was so close to this person that if her arms hadn't been tied, she could have reached out and touched that leering mask.

"Where are you taking us?" she asked, her voice hoarse and trembling.

The killer shot her a glance. The mask's eyes were cold and empty looking.

"To the lake."

The words shocked May to her core. She gasped in astonishment.

It was a woman speaking.

Her voice was strongly tinged with the flavor of Eastern Europe.

May felt utterly stunned to have learned this fact about the killer's identity, and as her mind raced back over the information she'd gathered, she made a guess.

"Are you Zinaida?" she asked.

Perhaps the woman hadn't died after all. Perhaps she really had disappeared and because they couldn't find her, the guards had been told to say she'd died, to scare the other workers.

The truck swerved sharply to the right as May spoke. The woman—the killer—turned to stare at her again. May guessed she was surprised. The mask gave nothing away.

"I am," she said.

"Zinaida, why are you going to the lake?"

"I could not drown that man in the beer vat. He got away from me and locked himself in the truck. So I am going to drive it into the lake. He will die there. We will all die. It is a fitting end."

Her voice sounded calm and resolute, as if she'd already accepted her fate.

May's heart accelerated.

"Wait, Zinaida! You don't have to do that."

"I do," she replied. Her hands were tight on the wheel. The truck hurtled around another sharp bend, tires skidding on the dusty ground.

"No. You don't have to do that. I'm a police officer. I'm going to arrest him. We need him. He's got important information."

"Being arrested is too good for that scum. He needs to die," she insisted through gritted teeth. "As for the police, how will they help? How did they help? You cared nothing for us! We were alone!"

May was starting to fit the puzzle pieces together, even though the picture they were creating was a terrible one. There must be a reason for this woman's intense anger, and for her to have done what she did.

"Did you know Laima? One of the other women told me she died a couple of years ago. Is this why you're doing it? Is it something to do with her?"

Zinaida stared at her again. May couldn't read the expression behind that grinning mask but she guessed the woman must be surprised.

But she was wrong.

When she spoke again, her voice was hoarse, tearful.

"She was my sister," she replied. She was sobbing now. "She was my sister, and she died a prisoner, abused, killed by one of the men they forced her to sleep with."

May felt filled with horror.

"Zinaida, I'm so sorry."

"She was beaten up, and then the man drowned her in the bathtub. That is how she died."

Now May understood why Zinaida was committing the murders this way. It was justice on her own terms, killing her targets the same way, beaten over the head and then drowned.

Despite her own dangerous situation, she felt tears prickling her own eyes. Losing a sister was the most shocking tragedy. She knew that only too well.

She deeply disapproved of Zinaida's actions, but in a tiny part of her mind, May could understand why this woman, traumatized and bereaved, had felt the need to get revenge.

She must have waited, planned, hidden. She'd been surviving for years. Perhaps she had a fake identity set up by now. Who knew?

But one thing May did know was that if she couldn't stop this woman from going ahead with her plans, they were all going to die. Horror filled her at the thought. What if she could not derail this woman from her murderous agenda?

She now recognized the road they were on, and it led down to one of the deeper parts of the lake. The road ended in a cul-de-sac just a few yards away from a steeply sloping bank and a fishing jetty. May's stomach twisted with terror at the thought of going over that steep bank and plunging down into the dark, cold, and deep waters of the lake.

She tried to imagine how long it would take them to drown. Would they suffer in the process, as they fought to get to the surface, or would it happen quickly?

She swallowed against a rising tide of panic and despair. How was she going to get out of this situation?

Perhaps the most important thing was to try and loosen her wrists.

The truck's cab was dark now as the sun had dropped below the horizon.

With all her strength, but trying not to let Zinaida see, May wrestled with the ties, doing her utmost to loosen them.

She wriggled as hard as she could, trying to undo the seatbelt and turn around to work at the knots holding her hands behind her back. She had to stop this woman before it was too late.

"Zinaida, please," she begged. "Please. Listen to me. I know you're hurt. I know you're angry. But you don't have to hurt anyone else. I know it's not what you want. You wanted to kill one man, not many people. You didn't want to hurt anyone else."

"You are wrong," Zinaida said. Her voice was shaking, but she sounded angry now. "You have no idea what you are talking about. I want to kill everyone I can get to."

May guessed she hadn't been able to get through Reed's security cohorts. Zinaida had picked her battles.

"I know, but you can't kill this man," she pleaded. "The police need him to get to the people who did this. To make sure everyone is punished. Even Reed," she added persuasively.

The woman hesitated for a moment, but then shook her head.

"I do not trust the police. You can be bribed. Juries are not predictable. This man deserves to die. He will suffer in the lake. He will drown. They will find him, and they will know what happened."

"No! You don't have to do this!" May pleaded. "I know you loved her. But you don't have to kill yourself too. There must be another way."

Zinaida did not reply. Her face was set like stone. She was driving fast, and the truck was bouncing over the bumpy road. In a moment, she would reach the end of the road and make a sharp turn.

"Zinaida, you can't do this," May said. "Please. Stop the truck. Rethink this. Let him suffer in prison. He will do that, I promise you."

For a moment, she felt the woman hesitate. She knew her words had gotten through to her. The truck's careening progress slowed.

"It'll be the right thing. Let me arrest him," May implored.

She wished she could see Zinaida's face. Hopefully she was close to making up her mind.

"Please," May said, hoping she was having an effect and that this terrifying ride could end before the truck reached the waters of the lake.

The truck slowed still further.

May felt a leap of hope. She'd done it. She'd managed to get Zinaida to rethink. They would all be saved. The truck would be stopped.

But then, Zinaida shook her head.

"Stop trying to make me change my mind," she yelled. "I will do what I need to do!"

She looked firmly ahead. And then she mashed her foot down on the accelerator. The truck leaped forward, engine screaming as they headed down the straight, downhill road to the lake.

"No!" Now May was the one shrieking in terror, fighting the ropes that held her arms behind her with all her might.

And as they flew over the rutted road, finally, May realized she'd done it. Her bonds were loose enough for her to tug her arms free. But the truck was already hurtling down the last stretch of road. In front of her, May could already see the point where the lights ended and the darkness of the water began.

She had just a few moments to try and save everyone from the disastrous consequences. She knew she had to do it. It was her only chance of sparing the lives of everyone in that truck. Even if it cost her own.

She put her hand down, reaching for her gun, deciding that she would threaten the other woman and if she had to, shoot her in the arm.

But her gun wasn't there. Zinaida had removed it.

With no more options left, May snapped open her seatbelt and lunged for the steering wheel.

CHAPTER TWENTY NINE

May grabbed hold of the wheel, desperately trying to veer the truck off course. But Zinaida was stronger than she looked. Her arms were tough and wiry. And she uttered a cry of rage at May's interference.

Now the truck was weaving dangerously, slewing from side to side as the two women fought.

May held on with all her strength, pulling it to the right, trying to veer the truck off its route.

But Zinaida was still fighting to hold the wheel straight. And with her other hand, she was throwing punches and blows at May. Her fist slammed into May's shoulder. Her nails raked May's face.

"Zinaida, please!" May cried, trying to grab her arm, but Zinaida yanked it away.

Then Zinaida swung at her again, this time hitting May hard in the face.

"Ow!" she cried, the impact stinging her cheek. She lunged for Zinaida's arm again and this time, managed to grab it, digging her fingers in as hard as she could.

"Don't do this, Zinaida. Please."

"No! I will do what I need to do! It is not your business. You do not understand!"

The vehicle was veering wildly left and right. It was impossible to control the wheel any longer. But they were still heading toward the lake.

May lashed out at Zinaida, hoping that she could somehow hit her away, or push her away, but the woman seemed immune to her blows. Zinaida was wedged into the corner of the truck, and May couldn't even reach the door to try and push her out.

May tugged at Zinaida's arm, trying to tug her off balance with every shred of strength she had. The truck swerved again, and May felt her heart race as the wheels lifted from the road. It was going to roll!

But then it righted itself and rattled on, faster than ever.

"Stop it, Zinaida," she said. "Stop it, please. I'm trying to save the other women. They're being rescued as we speak. I am trying to help. We need his testimony."

Zinaida's only reply was to try and slap May's face again. In response, May aimed a punch at her. It was hard and accurate, thudding into her side, but Zinaida didn't seem to feel it. She threw a punch right back at May and knocked her sideways.

May's head bashed against the door of the truck and for a few moments, the world went gray.

Then it brightened again, propelling her into a terrifying scenario.

May shrieked in fear.

The runaway truck was now accelerating over the water's edge. At high speed, it was curving out in a deadly arc that would take it down into these deep, cold waters. The descent was twisting her stomach with its speed. She could hear the engine's roar and see the lake's dark depths, waiting to swallow her.

But the driver's door was swinging open and Zinaida had gone.

At the very last second, her captor had jumped out and made her escape, leaving May to her fate.

*

The truck plunged into the lake. The impact felt as sharp and sudden as a car crash, and May was jolted in her seat. Water surged and foamed high in the air. The truck rolled violently to the left. She was horrified by how quickly it sank, with water streaming through the door that Zinaida had opened.

Panic rose in her throat but she forced it down. She could get out of that door, although it was now at the lower part of the steeply angled truck. Zinaida had left her a lifeline. She wasn't trapped. She could dive, swim through it, and find her way to the surface.

May took a deep breath. The waters were already at neck height, cold and clammy.

She dove down, swimming as strongly as she could toward the gap in the door, feeling utterly focused on saving herself. She was not going to become the killer's final victim. She was not!

She made it through the door, wriggling out of the narrow gap. Determinedly, May kicked for the surface of the lake.

With her lungs bursting, she reached it, gulping a huge breath of air.

She'd saved herself. She'd done it!

But then, with a clench of horror, she realized the truth. She didn't just have to save herself. She also had to rescue her witness. The ordeal was not over, and in fact, had only just begun.

Every second now counted. She had to dive down again, in time to get Lewis out of the now flooded truck.

May just hoped there was a corner of air left in the back of the truck, because otherwise, by now, he might have drowned.

Feeling cold terror clench her stomach at the thought, she turned back, gulped in the deepest possible breath, and plunged underwater again.

She felt her heart pound as she descended. She could feel her fear was ready to overpower her. What if she drowned? What if she was too late?

Her lungs were burning. Her fingers were numb, and she couldn't feel her legs anymore.

But she had to do this. She had to save him. May kicked as hard as she could. She had to get there.

She reached the truck and stared into the darkness. She could hear water sloshing, and could hear the truck now creaking and groaning as it settled further into the lake.

The keys, May remembered. She'd almost forgotten about them. Without the keys, she couldn't open the back of the truck. She grabbed the open door and pulled herself back into the cab, fumbling for them in the ignition.

There they were. She kept a tight hold of them because if she dropped these keys, she would never find them again.

Swimming out, she went to the back of the truck, which was completely underwater. Where was the keyhole? Which of the two keys would work? Down here in the dark and murky depths, it was all but impossible to figure out.

May found the handle more by touch than sight. She fumbled with the keys, realizing how cold her hands were. She almost dropped them as they slipped against the truck's paintwork, and her heart almost stopped with fright.

Clinging to the keys, she tried again to get them in. This one definitely didn't work. It must be the other one.

She managed to get it in and turned it, but the door wouldn't budge. She was exhausted. Her shoulders burned, her muscles felt like they were bursting with pain.

But she tried again. Turned and pulled. Harder. Giving it everything she had.

Why wouldn't it move? She needed to breathe. She needed to get back to the surface and get some air into her burning lungs.

If she didn't breathe, she would drown. But if she did breathe, she would be too late. Moment by moment, the truck was filling with water. Lewis would drown soon.

May's heart was pounding as she felt her limbs growing numb. She had reached her limit. She couldn't stay down here much longer. Just now, despite her efforts, she knew that she'd gasp in a gulp of water and she, too, would drown in these unfriendly depths.

But she had to rescue Lewis. She had to.

May tugged and twisted again, this time with all her might, feeling as if her head was about to burst and her lungs might explode.

This time the door opened.

It was dark, and she couldn't see a thing. But she could feel. She could feel the truck rocking, and moving down, deeper to the bottom.

She had to go deeper. She had to find him.

She reached out with her hands, feeling around, kicking further into the depths. Where was he? Where was he?

Her hands struck something cold and soft.

There was Lewis, slumped against the rear of the truck.

She grabbed Lewis's arm and pulled as hard as she could. His head lolled back as she dragged him toward her.

May's heart felt like it was going to burst as she struggled to get him out of there. But adrenaline was giving her the final surge of strength she needed.

She dragged him up and out. He was limp, unconscious, and probably already dead. May knew she was probably too late. But she had to try.

Dragging him behind her, aware that if she let go of him she would never find him again in time, May breasted the surface of the lake. She was coughing and choking now, her throat raw and her chest burning.

May gasped in a breath and coughed out the lake water in her lungs, then gulped in another breath, clutching on to Lewis's inert body as she lunged for the pier.

Then she heard Lewis splutter as well. She heard him cough and choke. He was alive.

May pulled herself up onto the pier, dragging him by his arms.

Choking and spluttering, weak and flailing, he crawled onto the pier.

Looking up, May saw the headlights of cars nearby and heard concerned voices. Apparently, the noise of the runaway truck had alerted locals and people were coming to help.

"Are you okay? What happened here?" a man shouted. A flashlight beam bobbed as he ran down toward them.

"We need police backup. Call nine one one, please!" May shouted.

She felt her belt. Zinaida had taken her gun away, but she still had the cable tie that could be used as an emergency handcuff.

Now that she knew Lewis was able to breathe on his own, she quickly dragged his hands behind him and secured him as tightly as she could with the cable tie.

"Wait!" His voice was hoarse and ragged, but outraged. "What are you doing?"

"You're coming in for questioning as soon as backup gets here," May told him, through teeth now chattering with cold. "You're wanted by local police and the FBI."

The horror in his face told her everything she needed to know about his guilt. Still coughing and spluttering, he struggled to pull himself to his feet. May kicked out his legs from under him and he fell back onto the pier.

"You're under arrest, and we're not letting you out of our sight until you're behind bars."

They had the suspect they needed to take the trafficking case further. But the killer was gone.

They needed to embark on a full-scale manhunt immediately. Comb the area, and get the FBI involved. But May had an uneasy feeling about Zinaida. After she'd jumped out of the moving truck and left them to their fate, May didn't know if they would ever find her again.

CHAPTER THIRTY

Back at the Fairshore police department, the entire building was abuzz. Police vans were parked outside. Media vans were converging.

FBI officials worked shoulder to shoulder with the local police as the suspects were processed.

May was still shivering, even though she'd managed to change into dry clothes and Owen had loaned her his spare jacket, which was a few sizes too big, but comforting and warm.

Despite being cold, she felt a warm glow of satisfaction. The teams had captured all the key people involved in the trafficking ring. All of them were now in FBI custody, including the kingpin of the operation, Lewis Brooks. With no notice or warning that their operation had been due to be raided, everybody had been on site and no evidence had been destroyed. There would be sufficient proof available to make sure all these evil people went into prison for many years.

From outside, she heard shouting and screaming as Bert Reed, who'd been in a cell in the local prison for the past two hours, was loaded up into a van, ready to be transported to the main FBI headquarters in Minneapolis. Lewis was currently being questioned by the FBI agents who'd flown in from Minneapolis, and would then be transferred to the same place.

This case was now out of their hands, but May couldn't have felt prouder that as a local team, not only had they gotten to the bottom of it, but they had also arrested Lewis Brooks.

She had no idea what would happen to the hotels. She guessed that the new hotel, the Lakeside Heights, would certainly go no further in its build. Perhaps it would be sold at some stage. At any rate, she felt glad that the campsites and surrounding restaurants would now have the chance to revive and thrive again. Freddy Featherstone would hopefully soon be back to full operational capacity.

There was only one missing piece to the puzzle and May shivered again as she thought about it.

The killer had disappeared.

Even though the police and FBI had immediately embarked on a manhunt of the area, it had brought no results. The woman who had slipped back like a shadow to inflict her revenge had disappeared again.

But May wasn't surprised. She'd managed to live like a shadow for years already.

She'd killed two people who were guilty of horrendous human rights violations, and who had blood on their hands. May didn't think she would kill again. Even though Zinaida was now wanted by the FBI, May doubted they would ever find her. She personally believed she'd procured an alternative ID a long time ago, and was going to melt back into her invisible life, satisfied that she'd meted out her own justice.

As a policewoman, May couldn't approve of this. But as a sister herself, she felt differently, even though she wasn't prepared to look at her mixed feelings too closely.

Had she been in Zinaida's situation, May wondered what she would have done.

Sheriff Jack bustled into the back office where May had just finished filling out the last of her reports.

"What a day this has been," he said. "We've got a media conference lined up for tomorrow. I think we've just about gotten through everything here now."

He gave May an approving nod. "I must commend you for your exceptional work on this. You didn't make the mistake of stopping too soon, but followed your instincts and made sure that you had investigated all the gaps in the case. By doing so you uncovered a massive criminal operation that was about to rapidly expand, and saved many lives. Your efforts have already received positive feedback and commendations from around the state and beyond. I believe the governor wants to thank you personally at a later stage."

"That's amazing." May couldn't have felt more proud at her boss's praise.

"The only missing piece in the puzzle is the escaped killer. But there is no direct evidence linking the woman you described to the crimes, or even any accurate information on her identity, as her passport was not among those we found. So from a logistical perspective we could not have taken this further, and we did everything we could to conclude the case. I think that with the entire trafficking ring in custody, the public will be reassured that the killings were an inside job and that no further killings will occur."

"Agreed," May said.

Sheriff Jack turned to her partner.

"Owen, you did a fantastic job. I am proud of the way you supported May, and your questioning of the hotel manager was impeccably done. You acted with courage and initiative."

May saw Owen stand taller in pride, and felt grateful for her boss's words of praise, and that he always took the time to commend each member of his team.

"I think it's time to knock off." Jack looked at his watch. "The press conference is at nine a.m. tomorrow. See you then."

May walked out, feeling proud and pleased, if still slightly wet and cold. She couldn't wait to get home and get warm.

"See you tomorrow morning. Well done," she said to Owen.

"It was a privilege to work with you on this, May," he said sincerely. "I couldn't ask for a better partner."

"Me, either," she said, smiling, feeling suddenly warmer.

They stood facing each other and then Owen did something surprising.

He leaned in and gave May a quick, strong hug.

It was unexpected, but May had to admit that his arms around her for that brief moment felt good. She hugged him back, hard. And then, without saying another word to each other, they climbed into their cars and set off for home.

May spent the five-minute trip reliving every moment of the intense day she'd just had. It had been a rollercoaster ride of note. She'd had to face her very worst fears, diving into the lake, rescuing trapped people, coming face to face with the killer.

She let out a deep breath as she pulled into her driveway. As she stopped the car, her eyebrows shot up in amazement.

Her sister was sitting on her front porch, in one of the two wicker chairs.

Kerry had a pack of beers with her, and a selection of takeout food. May's headlights gleamed over her blond hair.

She climbed out of her car feeling shocked.

"Kerry! What are you doing here?" she asked.

"We just wrapped up on our side. The criminals are all in custody in Minneapolis. So it's over to that branch now. I left half an hour ago, and thought you might need some food and drink."

"But where's Brandon?"

Kerry smiled. "He had to fly out to a meeting this afternoon. That's why we did breakfast. It was literally the only time available. And I thought I'd stay here tonight, rather than waking up the folks. I can sleep on your couch?"

"Okay," May said. That was fine with her. "I do have a spare bedroom."

"Let's go in. You must be freezing. Shall I get the fire going?"

141

May unlocked the front door and Kerry bustled in, whirling around the living room as she piled wood into the fireplace.

"That was an excellent case. What a raid! Getting those lowlifes under lock and key was one of the most satisfying experiences I've had, and the women were so grateful to be rescued. All of them thanked you. I told them it was your doing that they were now going to be safe. You handled this like a pro."

With the fire now crackling, she handed May a beer, put the takeout bag on the coffee table, sat down, and patted the couch beside her.

"Your sheriff told me you actually had to wrestle with the killer in a runaway truck heading for the lake. May, that sounds like something out of the movies!"

"I guess it was," May said.

"Tell me about it!" Kerry's eyes were shining.

For a brief, surprised moment, May saw actual admiration in them.

A weird thought occurred to her.

Thanks to the way her mother had always pitted the children against each other, was it possible that Kerry was jealous of her?

There was no reason to be. Kerry had been the golden child in every way. But thinking about it, May thought that it would explain some of her behavior.

Perhaps this case had allowed them to work on an equal footing, and taken away some of the perceived unfairness that each one felt about the other, however illogical it might be.

"Well, I woke up in the truck. It was roaring along, and my hands were tied behind my back, and the driver was accelerating along the back roads, wearing a Joker mask," May began.

"No way!" Kerry enthused, leaning forward.

May knew, with a happy feeling inside, that Kerry would listen to this entire story without any interruption or criticism. She would drink in every detail of May's thrilling experience. And then May wanted to hear a blow by blow account of the fascinating raid, with no details or omissions.

It was amazing to feel in harmony with her older sister.

But she couldn't help feeling a flash of regret that all three of them could not be sitting together on this balmy night.

Even though her relationship with Kerry felt as if it was starting to stabilize, the absence of Lauren would always leave a hole in her heart. She hoped that the permission to reopen the case would arrive soon.

EPILOGUE

The next day, May arrived at the Fairshore police department at eight-thirty. She hadn't had much sleep. She and Kerry had swapped war stories into the small hours. May felt tired, but happy.

As she rushed into the police department, ready to prepare for the press conference, Sheriff Jack called her name.

"May. I have some news for you. We've got the go-ahead to reopen your sister's case. The file is being sent today. I hope you find something that can help," he said, his tone at once hopeful and comforting.

May's heart leapt.

Finally, she was going to be able to relook into the confusing, conflicting circumstances of Lauren's disappearance. Nerves twisted inside her at what she might find.

In fact, she couldn't wait.

Now that she had the official go-ahead, she wanted to do what she'd been so tempted to do two days ago, as she'd stood in the evidence room, scenarios unfolding in her imagination.

Now, she had actual permission to open the box. And she wanted to have a quick look inside before the press conference began.

May took the key for the evidence room and hurried through. She unlocked the door and stepped into the cool, musty-smelling place.

Feeling breathless, she trod along the length of the room, past the quiet shelves.

There it was. The box she needed. She lifted it down from the shelf and placed it on the floor.

With shaking fingers, she gently teased the tape away and loosened it.

This was all that remained of her sister's movements and possessions on that fateful day. The only traces of it were here. It had happened so long ago. What hope did she have?

But May reminded herself firmly that there was always hope.

She took the box and opened the cardboard top. Then she moved it under a light and peered inside.

So little was there. Just a few items, all carefully bagged. Untouched for a decade, and now touched again by her shaking fingertips lifting them out. Underneath was the folded log of the items.

There were the tiny scraps of fabric from her blouse, stained with blood.

There was a button from Lauren's shirtsleeve, found in the same area. May remembered that now.

Her water bottle, with the traces of her saliva on it. That pink bottle had been found near the lake, a few yards away from the fabric.

And something else. What was this?

Puzzled, May lifted the bag and looked inside.

It was a key. A small metal key, the steel slightly discolored with age, grainy and gray. It was attached to a plastic key ring.

And on the key ring was scrawled an address, old and blurred and all but unreadable. Narrowing her eyes, she squinted at the lettering.

This was weird.

Had it been misfiled? she wondered. A key had never been mentioned. What was it for, and how had it even ended up here?

She stared at it, feeling shivers trail up and down her spine as she considered the possibility that maybe, just maybe, this would lead to something more. She needed to examine this blurred lettering more closely and if she did, surely there was a chance to work out what the address was. Perhaps a magnifying glass or a microscope might yield some answers as to what key it was, and what it opened.

She didn't dare to wonder if this might even unlock some of the mystery surrounding Lauren's disappearance. She had always suspected, deep inside, that there was more to it and that some questions had never been answered.

Had her sister's case been given up on too soon by the previous sheriff?

Putting the box carefully back on the shelf and hurrying out of the evidence room, ready for the press conference, May felt a sense of confidence flaming inside her. She knew she could do this. She resolved she was not going to let go this time. No matter what.

The key might mean nothing.

But then again, it could mean everything.

NOW AVAILABLE!

NEVER LIVE
(A May Moore Suspense Thriller—Book 3)

From #1 bestselling mystery and suspense author Blake Pierce comes a gripping new series: May Moore, 29, an average Midwestern woman and deputy sheriff, has always lived in the shadow of her older, brilliant FBI agent sister. Yet the sisters are united by the cold case of their missing younger sister—and when a new serial killer strikes in May's quiet, Minnesota lakeside town, it is May's turn to prove herself, to try to outshine her sister and the FBI, and, in this action-packed thriller, to outwit and hunt down a diabolical killer before he strikes again.

"A masterpiece of thriller and mystery."
—Books and Movie Reviews, Roberto Mattos (re Once Gone)

An after-prom party by the lake has gone horribly awry, with a teenage victim found dead on the shore.

May struggles to connect the dots, trying to reconstruct an evening that none of the partiers can remember. Did the party simply spiral out of control?

Or could this be the work a new killer?

A page-turning and harrowing crime thriller featuring a brilliant and tortured Deputy Sheriff, the MAY MOORE series is a riveting mystery, packed with non-stop action, suspense, jaw-dropping twists, and driven by a breakneck pace that will keep you flipping pages late into the night.

Future books in the series will be available soon.

"An edge of your seat thriller in a new series that keeps you turning pages! ...So many twists, turns and red herrings... I can't wait to see what happens next."
—Reader review (Her Last Wish)

"A strong, complex story about two FBI agents trying to stop a serial killer. If you want an author to capture your attention and have you guessing, yet trying to put the pieces together, Pierce is your author!"
—Reader review (Her Last Wish)

"A typical Blake Pierce twisting, turning, roller coaster ride suspense thriller. Will have you turning the pages to the last sentence of the last chapter!!!"
—Reader review (City of Prey)

"Right from the start we have an unusual protagonist that I haven't seen done in this genre before. The action is nonstop... A very atmospheric novel that will keep you turning pages well into the wee hours."
—Reader review (City of Prey)

"Everything that I look for in a book... a great plot, interesting characters, and grabs your interest right away. The book moves along at a breakneck pace and stays that way until the end. Now on go I to book two!"
—Reader review (Girl, Alone)

"Exciting, heart pounding, edge of your seat book... a must read for mystery and suspense readers!"
—Reader review (Girl, Alone)

Blake Pierce

Blake Pierce is the USA Today bestselling author of the RILEY PAGE mystery series, which includes seventeen books. Blake Pierce is also the author of the MACKENZIE WHITE mystery series, comprising fourteen books; of the AVERY BLACK mystery series, comprising six books; of the KERI LOCKE mystery series, comprising five books; of the MAKING OF RILEY PAIGE mystery series, comprising six books; of the KATE WISE mystery series, comprising seven books; of the CHLOE FINE psychological suspense mystery, comprising six books; of the JESSE HUNT psychological suspense thriller series, comprising twenty four books; of the AU PAIR psychological suspense thriller series, comprising three books; of the ZOE PRIME mystery series, comprising six books; of the ADELE SHARP mystery series, comprising fifteen books, of the EUROPEAN VOYAGE cozy mystery series, comprising four books; of the new LAURA FROST FBI suspense thriller, comprising nine books (and counting); of the new ELLA DARK FBI suspense thriller, comprising eleven books (and counting); of the A YEAR IN EUROPE cozy mystery series, comprising nine books, of the AVA GOLD mystery series, comprising six books (and counting); of the RACHEL GIFT mystery series, comprising six books (and counting); of the VALERIE LAW mystery series, comprising three books (and counting); of the PAIGE KING mystery series, comprising six books (and counting); and of the MAY MOORE suspense thriller series, comprising three books (and counting).

An avid reader and lifelong fan of the mystery and thriller genres, Blake loves to hear from you, so please feel free to visit www.blakepierceauthor.com to learn more and stay in touch.

BOOKS BY BLAKE PIERCE

MAY MOORE SUSPENSE THRILLER
NEVER RUN (Book #1)
NEVER TELL (Book #2)
NEVER LIVE (Book #3)

PAIGE KING MYSTERY SERIES
THE GIRL HE PINED (Book #1)
THE GIRL HE CHOSE (Book #2)
THE GIRL HE TOOK (Book #3)
THE GIRL HE WISHED (Book #4)
THE GIRL HE CROWNED (Book #5)
THE GIRL HE WATCHED (Book #6)

VALERIE LAW MYSTERY SERIES
NO MERCY (Book #1)
NO PITY (Book #2)
NO FEAR (Book #3

RACHEL GIFT MYSTERY SERIES
HER LAST WISH (Book #1)
HER LAST CHANCE (Book #2)
HER LAST HOPE (Book #3)
HER LAST FEAR (Book #4)
HER LAST CHOICE (Book #5)
HER LAST BREATH (Book #6)

AVA GOLD MYSTERY SERIES
CITY OF PREY (Book #1)
CITY OF FEAR (Book #2)
CITY OF BONES (Book #3)
CITY OF GHOSTS (Book #4)
CITY OF DEATH (Book #5)
CITY OF VICE (Book #6)

A YEAR IN EUROPE

A MURDER IN PARIS (Book #1)
DEATH IN FLORENCE (Book #2)
VENGEANCE IN VIENNA (Book #3)
A FATALITY IN SPAIN (Book #4)

ELLA DARK FBI SUSPENSE THRILLER
GIRL, ALONE (Book #1)
GIRL, TAKEN (Book #2)
GIRL, HUNTED (Book #3)
GIRL, SILENCED (Book #4)
GIRL, VANISHED (Book 5)
GIRL ERASED (Book #6)
GIRL, FORSAKEN (Book #7)
GIRL, TRAPPED (Book #8)
GIRL, EXPENDABLE (Book #9)
GIRL, ESCAPED (Book #10)
GIRL, HIS (Book #11)

LAURA FROST FBI SUSPENSE THRILLER
ALREADY GONE (Book #1)
ALREADY SEEN (Book #2)
ALREADY TRAPPED (Book #3)
ALREADY MISSING (Book #4)
ALREADY DEAD (Book #5)
ALREADY TAKEN (Book #6)
ALREADY CHOSEN (Book #7)
ALREADY LOST (Book #8)
ALREADY HIS (Book #9)

EUROPEAN VOYAGE COZY MYSTERY SERIES
MURDER (AND BAKLAVA) (Book #1)
DEATH (AND APPLE STRUDEL) (Book #2)
CRIME (AND LAGER) (Book #3)
MISFORTUNE (AND GOUDA) (Book #4)
CALAMITY (AND A DANISH) (Book #5)
MAYHEM (AND HERRING) (Book #6)

ADELE SHARP MYSTERY SERIES
LEFT TO DIE (Book #1)
LEFT TO RUN (Book #2)

LEFT TO HIDE (Book #3)
LEFT TO KILL (Book #4)
LEFT TO MURDER (Book #5)
LEFT TO ENVY (Book #6)
LEFT TO LAPSE (Book #7)
LEFT TO VANISH (Book #8)
LEFT TO HUNT (Book #9)
LEFT TO FEAR (Book #10)
LEFT TO PREY (Book #11)
LEFT TO LURE (Book #12)
LEFT TO CRAVE (Book #13)
LEFT TO LOATHE (Book #14)
LEFT TO HARM (Book #15)

THE AU PAIR SERIES
ALMOST GONE (Book#1)
ALMOST LOST (Book #2)
ALMOST DEAD (Book #3)

ZOE PRIME MYSTERY SERIES
FACE OF DEATH (Book#1)
FACE OF MURDER (Book #2)
FACE OF FEAR (Book #3)
FACE OF MADNESS (Book #4)
FACE OF FURY (Book #5)
FACE OF DARKNESS (Book #6)

A JESSIE HUNT PSYCHOLOGICAL SUSPENSE SERIES
THE PERFECT WIFE (Book #1)
THE PERFECT BLOCK (Book #2)
THE PERFECT HOUSE (Book #3)
THE PERFECT SMILE (Book #4)
THE PERFECT LIE (Book #5)
THE PERFECT LOOK (Book #6)
THE PERFECT AFFAIR (Book #7)
THE PERFECT ALIBI (Book #8)
THE PERFECT NEIGHBOR (Book #9)
THE PERFECT DISGUISE (Book #10)
THE PERFECT SECRET (Book #11)
THE PERFECT FAÇADE (Book #12)

ONCE GONE (Book #1)
ONCE TAKEN (Book #2)
ONCE CRAVED (Book #3)
ONCE LURED (Book #4)
ONCE HUNTED (Book #5)
ONCE PINED (Book #6)
ONCE FORSAKEN (Book #7)
ONCE COLD (Book #8)
ONCE STALKED (Book #9)
ONCE LOST (Book #10)
ONCE BURIED (Book #11)
ONCE BOUND (Book #12)
ONCE TRAPPED (Book #13)
ONCE DORMANT (Book #14)
ONCE SHUNNED (Book #15)
ONCE MISSED (Book #16)
ONCE CHOSEN (Book #17)

MACKENZIE WHITE MYSTERY SERIES
BEFORE HE KILLS (Book #1)
BEFORE HE SEES (Book #2)
BEFORE HE COVETS (Book #3)
BEFORE HE TAKES (Book #4)
BEFORE HE NEEDS (Book #5)
BEFORE HE FEELS (Book #6)
BEFORE HE SINS (Book #7)
BEFORE HE HUNTS (Book #8)
BEFORE HE PREYS (Book #9)
BEFORE HE LONGS (Book #10)
BEFORE HE LAPSES (Book #11)
BEFORE HE ENVIES (Book #12)
BEFORE HE STALKS (Book #13)
BEFORE HE HARMS (Book #14)

AVERY BLACK MYSTERY SERIES
CAUSE TO KILL (Book #1)
CAUSE TO RUN (Book #2)
CAUSE TO HIDE (Book #3)
CAUSE TO FEAR (Book #4)
CAUSE TO SAVE (Book #5)

CAUSE TO DREAD (Book #6)

KERI LOCKE MYSTERY SERIES
A TRACE OF DEATH (Book #1)
A TRACE OF MURDER (Book #2)
A TRACE OF VICE (Book #3)
A TRACE OF CRIME (Book #4)
A TRACE OF HOPE (Book #5)